THE WATER MILL

A GHOST STORY

CHARLOTTE WEBB

NENE PUBLISHING

CHAPTER 1
THE NEW HOME

Abbie pulled the family car to a halt behind the moving van and got out slowly, surveying their new home. The midday sunlight had been bright and cheerful at the top of the road, but a dense chill lingered in the shadows of the woods surrounding the converted mill. Their new grounds—far more extensive than she knew what to do with, they hadn't even had a garden back in London, hemmed in with a thick tumble of yew bushes, their blood-red berries glinting at her through the undergrowth. Some neighbour's cat yowled and hissed faintly in the distance, unseen, but it didn't come close enough to greet them. The canopy of the autumnal trees, still clinging onto the last of their dying leaves, rustled above her, blocking out the blue beyond. Abbie glanced back to the gate at the top of the sloping driveway behind them. It creaked mockingly on its hinges. Her daughter Sophie hadn't latched it properly. Fancifully, she thought it seemed to be beckoning them back.

Abbie resisted the urge to pull her cardigan more closely around herself. It never did any good to give in to superstitious nonsense. It was just the quiet that was disconcerting, probably. She'd never lived anywhere that wasn't accompanied by the drone of traffic and the symphony of squabbling pedestrians before.

"Oh, bit brisk here, isn't it?" John gave her a winning smile and a peck on the cheek as he jumped out of the driver's side of their borrowed van. "It's like our own little microclimate. Never mind, it'll do the new veg patch good. I've read that sprouts and taters like a good sharp frost to grow."

Abbie smiled indulgently. John always had such a comfortable, stolid presence about him. He was determined to start a vegetable patch and compost heap in their great "escape to the country". Earn his rural credentials, he said. Prove he wasn't just another city-slicker who couldn't hack it. She was sure it would be replaced by his next great passion project soon enough.

He always had a hungry soul. That was what had first drawn her to him, and that's what made him such an evocative painter. He was always desperate to taste all life had to offer and pin it down in thick-spread hues and pigments.

"Renovations first, garden second," she said firmly. "That was the deal. I'm not going to be left to do all the DIY alone this time. I only agreed to buy this house on the condition that you actually *helped* me."

He chuckled. "You know I'm much more of an ideas man."

"Yes," she said dryly. "It was your idea to buy a house that had been abandoned for seven years."

"Oh, ye of little faith. You're just looking at it as it is, you need to start seeing it's *potential.* Exactly what it could be!" He swiped his arm across vista in front of the large grey stone building, just as if he were a shmoozing estate agent. "You're just seeing the charmingly rustic, sturdy stone walls—"

"Which means the house will be cold," she interjected with a smile.

"And original windows."

"Small, and single glazed."

"And the attached stable which already came with planning permission to convert into a garage."

"We need to finish the interior before we worry about the car!"

"You're not seeing the beautifully decorated family home, or the little art gallery where we display our work, or the personal studio we can work in every day without needing to commute." He swept her up in his arms and kissed her again. "A studio, Abs," he murmured, his eyes sparkling. "A real studio we can share for just the two of us. No more rental fees, no more sharing with other artists, or finding that our area has been double booked. A space of our own. A place we can let our imaginations and creative urges run wild. And just look at this place! You have to admit it's beautiful. I can feel the inspiration filling me already."

He twirled her around their new driveway, and she let herself be swayed, giggling. He always managed to get his own way in the end. And it was true that most of the heavy lifting of the building conversion had been done already. The old mill had been turned into a mostly habitable, if not entirely comfortable home, and only needed cosmetic tidying.

Still...

Pulling herself out of his arms, she stumbled to a halt before the water. She eyed the great mill pond by the side of their new house dubiously. The algae-kissed depths reflected the branches of the trees looming over them, and the disjointed shapes created the strangest illusion that it was rippling, though no breeze disturbed them. That water was deep. She could almost feel the chill rising from its near-black depths, even from here. There was a peculiar, muted silence lingering over the waters, as if it was shrouded, somehow, and she couldn't shake the eerie feeling that it was watching her right back. She tried to look away but found that she couldn't tear her eyes from the glistening water surface. It seemed to be hauling her in, though her feet wouldn't move. Fear choked her abruptly. The cold prickle of sweat pearled on her skin. Ridiculously, it almost felt like she was in the water itself. As if it was closing in around her, flooding over her head, stinging her eyes, rushing down her throat—

"Love?"

She startled at John's hand on her elbow. His eyes, just as warm and comforting as always, broke the spell and she gave him a strained smile.

"Are you alright?" he murmured.

She tried to nod but couldn't. It felt too much like a lie. Irresistibly, her gaze was lured back to the edge of the water. It was almost certainly her imagination, but it seemed closer than before, though whether she had moved towards it, or it had moved towards *her,* she couldn't say. Her fingers clawed through John's coat, as if hoping to dredge up and steal some of his sturdy commonsense.

"Was it sensible of us to buy a house with such a deep pool attached to it?" she said. "What if the children fall in and drown? I could never live with myself."

John laughed at that. "It's a little late for second-thoughts now. We've already exchanged keys!" He slung an affable arm around her shoulders, and she shrugged herself into his side, feeling the reassuring patter of his heartbeat under her eager hand. "Besides, the kids are both in double digits now. They're not babies, and they know how to swim. They'll be fine. Anyway, I've sometimes thought it might be good to throw Sophie into a pond or two. Get her out of her teenage moods."

Abbie elbowed him at that. Sophie was in earshot, and, had she not had her headphones in, she almost certainly would have heard.

He just grinned unrepentantly. "Look, it's been a long day, and we're all tired. What do you say we go in and unpack the kettle? Thing's will look a lot better after a nice cup of tea."

"They call it a *paned* here, Dad," ten-year-old Max piped up, balancing his way along a fallen log. His gangly arms—strangely disproportionate after his last growth spurt—waved wildly as he tried to keep his balance. "I read about it in a guidebook when you first told us we were going to move. If we're going to live in Wales, you need to learn Welsh. We've got to fit in with the locals."

"Righto, son. We'll leave all the translating to you then, shall we?" He smirked over at Abbie and leant in, lowering his voice. "You were worried about his transition here too, weren't you? And look how well he's adjusted already. Maybe, just *maybe,* you worry too much. But if bothers you that much, I'll put a fence up around the millpond just as soon as I can with a whacking great sign that says 'Keep out! Absolutely no drowning!' Will that do you?"

Abbie glanced at the pool again. It might be her imagination, but those eerie, windless ripples seemed to be moving faster than ever, as if the mere sound of that word had excited them.

Or angered them.

She shuddered. "Oh, don't be flippant, John."

But he wasn't listening.

"Of course, I'm starting to think Sophie has forgotten how to read," he teased loudly enough so that Sophie could hear it, even over her headphones. "I can't remember the last time she picked up a book. But maybe if I made a dance video and put it on the internet, she might notice."

Sophie rolled her eyes so hard that Abbie could almost hear them swivelling in their sockets.

Abbie took a deep breath and collected herself. John was right. She'd always been too imaginative. That was why she became an artist in the first place, wasn't it? To try to sculpt out and pin down some of the nightmares revolving inside her over-fertile brain.

"You're right," she said aloud. "A cup of tea would do us all good. Sorry, Max, *paned*. You grab the bag from the back of the car and dig out the kettle and mugs, and I'll get the sheets and sleeping bags set up in the bedrooms. Then, at the very least, we can go to sleep once the unpacking is done." She glanced at the pool again. "It'll all look better in the morning. It usually does."

THE NIGHT HAD FALLEN in earnest by the time that the last of the boxes had been unceremoniously dumped in the middle of their new floors. They had tried to downsize before the move, but judging by the cardboard castle now erected around them, clearly, they had not been stringent enough.

Though she'd already had four cups of tea, and they had polished off the packet of chocolate hobnobs between them, Abbie was both exhausted and famished.

She slumped on the old sofa. "We're never moving again."

"You say that every time." John smirked, flopping beside her.

"I mean it this time. You can just bury me right here on this sofa." She snuggled into his side. "Takeaway for dinner?"

"Your wish is my command." He grunted slightly as he wriggled his phone out of his jeans pocket. The app wouldn't open. The loading disk spun in endless, futile circles in the centre of the screen, mocking them.

John cursed softly under his breath, holding his phone up and wiggling it around wildly in the universal gesture for *where is the damned signal?*

"No luck?" Abbie groaned, scrubbing her eyes. "We could do it the old-fashioned way and phone them?"

"How? We can't look up the phone number with no internet," he reminded her with a grimace. "We might have found the one downside to our idyllic country retreat."

"Great! Perfect! So not only did I get dragged away from my friends, I can't even message them anymore!" Sophie threw her hands skywards dramatically.

"You'll get your Oscar in the post, Soph," John retorted. He held up his useless phone to his ear. "Hello, Hollywood? Why, yes, she *is* available for the role of deprived and neglected child."

"Urgh!" Sophie kicked over the nearest box, slamming the door behind her as she stormed out into the dark rooms beyond.

Abbie elbowed him. Antagonising Sophie now wouldn't do any good. She heaved herself out of the sofa with a groan. "I'll pop to the village and grab some dinner in person. And tomorrow, we'll order one of those wi-fi extension things you can plug in. Sophie's right, we can't live here long term with no internet. It's not the Middle Ages."

"Oh, I don't know. It might be an adventure. Besides, it could be nice being off the grid. Unreachable. We'd be like spies, wouldn't we, kid?" He winked at Max.

"Can I come with you, Mum? I want to make sure the pizza people don't mix the peppers and the ham pieces. It's pepper on one side, ham on the other. They can't touch, otherwise they're gross and contaminated." He had already squeezed his coat and shoes on, heading for the door.

"At least one of us is still cheerful," she murmured to John. "Go and make up with Sophie whilst we're gone, won't you? Life is hard enough at sixteen without any major life changes. She's struggling right now. A little compassion wouldn't go amiss."

She went to follow Max out, but John caught her around the waist one last time. His flippant grin had turned into a deep and earnest smile.

"I know you're worried about her," he murmured, stroking a strand of bobbed chestnut hair out of her face and tucking it behind her ear. "I know you're worried about all of us, but we're doing this for our family. There are opportunities here we never could have given them back in a cramped two-bedroom rented flat in the city. It's going to be good for our family, Abs. It's going to be *great*."

And as he pressed a deep and hungry kiss to her lips, she almost found herself believing him.

EVEN JOHN HAD to admit that their new house felt cavernous and eerily quiet once Abbie and Max had driven away. He lingered by the small, draughty window, watching them go. The last blinding flash of their headlights had chuntered up the gravel slope and faltered only briefly as Abbie got out to fumble with the gate—*perhaps when funds are a little less tight, we can invest in one of those fancy electric ones*—and then they were away. And John was left in their new sitting room. Alone.

The temperature seemed to drop a few degrees. He'd never really got into the habit of keeping his own company. Abs, now, she could happily be alone all day long, but John thrived on people; on their voices, on their laughter and their stories. He'd never really got on well on his own.

He ran a hand up the back of his neck, surveying the carnage of half-unpacked boxes and badly arranged furniture around him. This was the most habitable room of the house right now, and it was still damp and mouldy. The seals around the windowpanes were almost a solid black as the mould spread there, and the speckles of grey had already tattooed the plasterwork beside them. It would take a full bottle of bleach to scrub them clean now, he was sure.

The confident smile he always kept firmly hoisted into place for Abbie and the kids' sake slipped slightly.

What have we got ourselves into?

John had never considered himself a religious man, but he found himself praying fervently that he hadn't dragged his entire family into the biggest mistake of their lives. Estate agent pictures were prone to exaggerate the truth, of course, but as they had driven down the slope this afternoon, he couldn't help but think that the house was in a far worse state than he'd remembered it. Abbie always accused him of unfounded optimism. He was starting to think she might be right. The converted mill that he had remembered from the tour had been brighter and warmer, the floorboards less creaking, the windows less cracked. The mill pond less ominously murky.

He glanced over at it instinctively. You could just about see the edge of it from the window here, stretching out before the front of the house. It ran all along one side of the house, next to the room they'd designated as their studio-to-be. The old mill race ran along the side of the house too—more ornate than functional now. That had been one of the things that had first drawn John in, actually, the existing 'original features of the charming period home'. Well, that and the cost, of course. It had seemed too good to be true.

In fact, it had all just made so much *sense* back in London. He had been able to see it all before him so clearly; the children free-ranging in their sprawling garden, no longer constantly tied to their screens. The dinners made with vegetables that they'd grown themselves, maybe even with eggs from their own chickens in due course. The local pub where he and Abbie would chat and laugh with the regulars. The dog they would adopt, who would lounge beside the log burning stove they would light with kindling from their own trees. And the studio he and Abs could work in, side by side, every day, filling the small gallery they would build up there on that empty patch of land on the far side of the garden. And it all seemed so tantalisingly close now, right within reach of his outstretched fingertips...

So why am I doubting now?

He wiped a hand over the condensation laced windowpane with a sigh. His gaze drifted irresistibly back to the pool at the side of the house once more. It looked even darker than before, reflecting the impenetrable blackness of the night around them.

Not a streetlight in sight to alleviate the gloom. I'll have to remember to put an outside light up. It's dangerous otherwise.

He added it to the bottom of his very long mental list.

The water glinted at him in the cloud-hazed starlight. He took half a step back, and then laughed at his own silliness. He didn't usually spook easily, but by the veiled glow of the moon it did seem a little otherworldly. The surface was sheening, almost greasily, and was so black that it seemed fathomless—as if it carried on going down and down until it met the very gateway of hell.

He shuddered and pulled himself together.

No, wild imaginative fantasies are Abbie's speciality. I'll leave them to her. And just think what sculptures she'll make living here!

Her last piece, *The Goblin Merchant,* had been a terrifying figure, lean limbed, leering, cat-faced and tailed, formed entirely from pewter moulded into the shapes of apple cores and welded together as a tribute to Christina Rossetti's *Goblin Market.* Like all the pieces Abbie was growing so famous for, it had been both spectacular and utterly, captivatingly creepy—a thing plucked directly from the twisted nightmares she was so prone to. It had also sold for enough money to round off their carefully saved deposit on this place, though perhaps a true artist ought not to think of such pecuniary matters.

If she could be similarly inspired whilst they were here, their dream garden-gallery could be built in no time at all...

He glanced up to the enticingly empty space on the far edge of the driveway. He could almost see the new building sprouting up there before his eyes, a narrow tangle of rooms leading, labyrinth-like in confusing spirals, twisting back and forth on top of each other until the visitors were lost in a world of art. A world where they could detach themselves from reality and become fully immersed, for a fleeting moment or two, in a world where everything was captivating, intentional and extraordinary. A far cry from the mundanities of everyday life. Art that he and Abbie had made, of course, and which would be for sale at respectable fee...

He smirked to himself for a moment then.

Abs is right. I must stop living in the future. We're a long way from that yet.

He rubbed his face forcefully with a small sigh. He'd best go and deal with Sophie. Abbie wouldn't be long and she'd chew his ear off if he hadn't smoothed things over with their firstborn by the time she got back. He whistled loudly as he left and he didn't really know why, except he had a sudden, irrepressible urge to fill the thick silence sludging around him. His footsteps echoed loudly, and he told himself not to look over his shoulder. There would be nothing there. He was alone.

But the shadow of the millpond haunted him out of the room, all the same.

The corridors beyond were even icier than the sitting room had been, if that was possible. He hadn't figured out how the central heating worked yet. Or even *if* it still worked. That was no guarantee after seven years unoccupied. He shivered again and then clicked his tongue.

You're getting worse than Abs, he chided himself. *It's just the old animal part of your brain, that's all. No matter how enlightened we get in this civilised age, the monkey brain still screams danger in the dark.*

And this all sounded very logical, but it didn't wipe away the fear prickling at the back of his neck.

He called for his daughter, but only the creak of the mill wheel replied in the silent house. He walked a little quicker, though he couldn't quite say why.

Sophie wasn't in her new room, or in the bathroom getting washed up, or even in the kitchen, on a futile hunt for food, but eventually he found a small crack of light seeping out from the new studio, warm and inviting. His chest loosened slightly. He pushed the door open with a creak.

Sophie was huddled in the corner. She didn't look up.

"Knock knock," he said softly, leaning against the door frame.

She didn't raise her head. It was still resting on her knees, which were tightly scrunched up to her chest, her arms clasping tightly around them to keep herself bundled up as small as she could be. From the single lightbulb swinging from the ceiling, her shadow swelled up against the wall where the inner spokes of the waterwheel sat. It ran across the rusted metal spiked cogwheels clinging to the stone walls, and was fractured out of shape by the lumps and crags transforming her silhouette into a strange, misshapen monster. Her breath, ragged and gasping, sounded oddly raspy in the echoing acoustics of the empty room, as if she had been transformed into an old lady in the mere minutes they'd been apart.

She's been crying.

Sophie had been a little... *temperamental*... of late, but she'd never been prone to crying before, even in the midst of her hormone riddled teen angst.

He licked his lips uneasily. "Mum's coming back soon with the pizza," he tried, "and she's said we'll get the wi-fi sorted first thing in the morning. Your friends won't forget you, love. I promise. How could they?"

She didn't move.

He stepped inside and crouched down beside her. His shadow stretched out too, engulfing hers until she was smothered in the shade of it. "I know it's been a lot. It's been a lot for me too."

"We didn't have to come!"

He bit back a sigh and tried to adopt his most understanding tone. "There's a better life here. We're just going to have to fight for it a little bit."

She looked up at him then with red, bloodshot eyes, and the rasping, old lady instantly disappeared. Before him was the tiny girl who had begged for just one more bedtime story, who giggled when he made her bubble beards in the bath, who had cuddled up on his lap when the nightmares came.

Your problems used to be so easy to solve, Soph. When did you grow up so much? When did I stop being the infallible hero who could chase away every bad thing in your life?

He held out his arms and she fell into them, sniffling her way into calmness again. After a few quivering breaths, she pulled herself free again and jutted her chin up with that defiance she'd had, ever since her toddler years.

"Alright, Dad. Talk me through your grand vision then," she said, wiping her eyes. And John had to laugh, for that was Abbie's phrase, hiding there in Sophie's mouth.

He got obediently to his feet. He could see it all coming to life before him, even now. He strode around the frigid room, waving his arms as if he could conjure up the vision through sheer will power.

"These big mill stones in the corner," he waved at the large, rugged circles piled up in place. "I thought we'd make them a feature piece, something to talk about in the new gallery we're going to build out on the front of the garden, you understand. I said tables for the visitors, but your mother said they'd be too heavy for that, so maybe stepping stones, all the way to entrance."

Sophie rose to look at them. She ran her hands along their rough surface and then sucked in a sharp breath as a jagged edge grazed her. She scowled, popping her finger into her mouth to stem the pinprick of blood there and sloped to the back wall, as if scurrying out of harm's reach lest it attacked her again. She waved at him to continue.

"And here, along this wall, this is where the cupboards will go, for the supplies," he added, gesturing to it. "There's no natural light back here, but that won't matter if it is just for the cupboards. This half is going to be your mother's sculpture zone, I've allocated her slightly more space than me, because you know she likes to spread out. And where you are, that is going to be my painting area," he said, gesticulating towards her. He stood back, his hands on his hips, surveying it with satisfaction, already imaging the easels lined up in a row, the paint drips speckling the floor.

Sophie tilted her head to one side thoughtfully considering the shadowy space she lurked in. "I thought you needed good natural light for painting? There's none of that back here. Why don't you go near the front by that small window."

"A window that size wouldn't provide enough light anyway," John pointed out.

"It would give more light than this solid wall, surely?" she asked. She patted it with her injured hand, and John tutted as he saw the small scrape on her finger smearing blood across the damp and mouldy walls. She ought to get some antiseptic cream on that before she did herself an injury.

"Well, there's the beauty of the thing, love. We're going to knock out half the back wall and turn the whole thing into floor to ceiling windows." He slung an arm over her shoulder, beaming. "It'll almost be like being outside, right in nature itself. The whole room will be *flooded* with light. It will be great."

"If you say so, Dad," she said, somewhat dubiously. "Isn't the place listed though? A building this old surely would be. Wouldn't building work like that go against regulations?"

"It probably should be listed," he admitted. "But the estate agents have said it isn't. It must have been missed by the inspectors who run that sort of thing—I suppose they can't get around to everyone at once and here, in the backend of nowhere, it must have just slipped through the net. I'm not going to tell them if you won't." He winked at her.

She laughed then—glorious sound! He didn't think he'd heard her laughing for months now, not since he and Abbie had sat the kids down to tell them that their offer had been accepted, and they were all going to be moving away for a grand adventure.

It's all going to be alright. She'll come around. We can be happy here too.

But from outside there was a shriek. A squeal of tyres. A roar of gravel. And a splash.

John's heart leapt to his throat as the watery echoes seemed to reverberate around the still room far too loudly—as if the water were dripping off the ceilings in this very room, all around them.

"Abbie! Max!"

He sprinted from the room, Sophie hot on his heels. Wrenching the door open, he spilled out into the night, still screaming their names.

The moonlight cast the whole scene into sharp relief, as if it were a tableau in a play. The front wheels of their car were buried in the front of the millpond, the back wheels spinning in the air, off the floor completely. Abbie, pale, shaken, had already thrown the driver's door open and had waded to the backseat. She was hauling Max from the booster seat he resented so much, burying him in her arms. He could see her hands trembling, even from here.

He was with her in seconds, pulling them both up to the shore. The water was so cold on his ankles that it stung, and it felt like it seeped in right through to the bone.

"You're hurt? What happened?" he demanded tersely.

She fell onto his chest, weeping, still clutching onto Max. "I'm so sorry. It was dark, and I'm not used to that steep driveway yet, and I'm so tired. I just lost control and I—"

"It's OK," he said, holding her tightly. She was corpse cold, and her breath rose between them in shivering mists. "As long as no one is hurt, that's the main thing." He tried to force a grin to his lips, but he wasn't sure how convincing it was. "Come on, Max, into the house you go. Did you rescue the pizza?"

"They didn't have a pizza shop here! They only had a fish and chip shop!" Max sounded more affronted about this than his near-death experience and John had to laugh.

"Right, well, you go in and see if you can unpack the plates and cutlery, and I'll see if I can rescue our dinner."

But Abbie clung onto his arm. "Don't go in that pond, John, it's not worth it."

"We need to eat, Abbie."

But Abbie had glanced at Max's disappearing back, already heading back to the safety of the well-lit indoors.

"I didn't just lose control of the car," she hissed, still not relinquishing his sleeve. "I saw something! It swooped across the front of the car. I skidded to avoid it and headed straight for the millpond."

"A bird, probably. Maybe an owl or something."

"No. It was a shadow. Large. Like a... a person, or something." Her eyes fixed up on his, and they were frantic with genuine terror. Wild, raw and petrified. "It was like it was trying to chase me away. Like it wanted me to crash."

Monkey brains don't like the dark, he reminded himself again. But whether or not it was real, it was real to *Abbie,* that was clear enough.

"Alright," he said softly. "We'll leave the car and the dinner for now. We'll all have another cup of tea and go straight to bed, and we'll find a café in the morning for a proper fry up breakfast to make up for it, how about that?"

"I'm not mad!" she said defensively, though he hadn't accused her of anything.

He captured her and kissed her softly beneath the moonlight. "I don't think you're mad," he said. "I think you're overwrought and over-tired. Sleep deprivation is a real thing and it plays cruel tricks on the brain. Do you remember how weird things got when the kids were newborns? I kept trying to put the milk in the washing machine instead of the fridge. Do you remember that?"

She snorted weakly, and the fearsome rigidity of her muscles loosened a notch. He stroked the hair away from her face.

"You've been worried about this move for so long," he murmured. "It's a big, stressful endeavour that has given you too many sleepless nights already and it is sure to give you a few more before the end. Your brain just short-circuited for a moment, that's all."

She closed her eyes, her head dropped down onto his chest softly. He stroked her hair again until she loosened a little more.

"Yeah. Maybe," she conceded at last, pulling herself away. But she wouldn't meet his eyes, nor would she glance in the direction of the millpond, staring straight ahead towards the front door as they hurried towards it.

The waterwheel creaked and splashed softly in the dark, echoing out into the night.

CHAPTER 2
A VILLAGE IN FEAR

All of the old curtains had been taken away by the previous owners—which was probably just as well, or they'd have rotted away by now anyway—so it was the cold light of dawn that woke them the next morning. The air was arctic, the cold crunching in Abbie's temples like a migraine. The prospect of unzipping her sleeping bag seemed dire indeed.

"At least you had the foresight to suggest them," John murmured beside her on the mattress sprawling across the floor. Their old bedframe had been disassembled and taped back into its old IKEA box, lounging against the wall waiting for them. He shuffled closer to her and she worm-wiggled into his side. "We'll get the heating up and running today, and I've phoned a handyman to come around and reassemble all the beds at once. He's due at lunchtime. By this evening, it'll be more like a real home, and less like camping in your own bedroom." He stretched theatrically, dislodging her. "Come on. There's bound to be a café in the village. Sausage, bacon and eggs are calling my name."

"We might need to replace the locks on the doors and windows too. I'm not sure they catch properly anymore," she murmured. "I think a stray cat got in last night. I could hear it hissing and spitting for hours."

He grinned at her. "Well, the poor little thing probably just wanted somewhere warm to sleep. You wouldn't be hard-hearted enough to oust a poor mangy mog into the cold, would you?"

As long as it's the only uninvited guest that slips through the window...

Despite Abbie's warnings, John waded into the pond before they left to reverse the car out again. It spluttered and dripped as it crunched its way back to dry land—and who knew what state the engine would be in after a night in the pond—but it still seemed to work, so that was something. John brought out the old fish and chips still abandoned on the front seat. The local newspaper that had been wrapped around them was a couple of days old, still complaining that the Senedd wouldn't hear formal complaints about the closures of the rural schools with a photo of glowering parents with placards. *No justice for innocent pupils,* the headline declared dramatically. Abbie just had time to read the first line, '*With a record number of school closures in rural communities, home schooling is now on the rise,*" when he lobbed the whole thing into the middle of the millpond. The water crashed upwards, disturbing the algae and pondweeds. Shadows shifted darkly beneath the surface of the rippling waves.

"An offering for the fishes from your magnanimous new owners," he declared loudly, making Max snort and even Sophie rolled her eyes with half a smile. "Feast well and think of us."

The white glint of the newspaper faded slowly as it sank into the murky darkness and Abbie grabbed hold of her children's hands. She couldn't resist one last glance over her shoulder as she hurried them away. The ripples still edged out in ever widening circles towards the shore of the pond, gently, slowly, inevitably washing their way towards her.

. . .

THE VILLAGE CAFÉ had not been redecorated in over a decade, if Abbie was any judge. But as the charges apparently hadn't been updated in all that time either, they probably shouldn't complain about it. The tables were a little greasy for her taste (and she dreaded to think what the state of the kitchen would be—a health and safety inspector's nightmare, no doubt) but John ordered four large breakfasts enthusiastically and she didn't want to ruin the mood.

"I won't call them a Full English here, eh?" he joked with the middle-aged lady behind the counter, whose expression didn't change at all.

An old man at the next table eyed them with undisguised curiosity. "Holidayers?" he guessed.

"No, we're here to stay," John said merrily. "Just moved into the old mill yesterday, in fact."

Perhaps it was Abbie's imagination, but she thought that several of the patrons shared dark looks with each other. An awkward silence bloomed through the oily air.

"Don't want any more outsiders coming to clog up your pretty village, eh?" John joked. "Don't worry, we fully intend on assimilating, don't we son?" He clapped a hand on Max's shoulder. Max looked up briefly from his book, decided nothing interesting was happening, and turned back to its pages without comment.

"The mill? That place must have been empty for well over a decade now," the café owner muttered, slopping their plates down in front of them. The sausages were very overcooked, and the eggs were a little runny, but the old, cracked plates were certainly stuffed to bursting. Abbie's stomach turned a little, just looking at it. She'd never be able to eat it all. She hoped that wouldn't offend their new neighbours.

"Seven years, the estate agent said," John said cheerily.

"That's right, Mari, there were those developers came by a few years back to do it up, but they only lasted a month or two," piped up a bottle-dye red-haired woman in the corner, nursing her mug of tea.

"Maybe it don't need doing up. Maybe it just needs leaving alone," the old man said darkly. "There's been accidents enough over that way, haven't there? We ain't looking to have any more."

"That's enough of that, Mr Edwards," Mari said, plonking two more cups of strong tea on the table alongside the heavily piled plates. "Best not to speak about that kind of thing, I reckon. Least said soonest mended."

"All I'm saying is there's a reason the young folks don't stay around here for long now," he muttered, turning back to his own bacon butty with a grunt. "Only us old folks with nowhere else to go risk staying."

"The young folk don't stay because they don't build any new homes for the young people to buy, and there's no jobs left for them to do!" the red-haired woman said hotly. "My Rhiannon and Dafydd lived here all their lives. She's already talking about moving away once she's finished at the university of hers, just so she can find a job. And what's the betting that Dafydd will have to do the same once he's finished school?"

"We don't need to bring politics into it all, Cerys," Mari said, back at her sentry position behind the till.

John raised his eyebrows gleefully at Abbie. "Looks like we stumbled our way into an episode of Scooby Doo," he whispered. "The crotchety old locals are inventing supernatural 'accidents' to keep the outsiders away. We're going to have fun here, I think."

Fun. Only John would see it that way.

But she smiled back at him anyway. He never

listened to reason. She learnt long ago to save her breath.

John turned to Mr Edwards. "You've lived here all your life too, I suppose."

Mr Edwards eyed him warily and nodded once, sharply.

John gave him his widest, warmest grin. "You'll be able to recommend a good builder for us then? I had a look before we moved, but I couldn't find any on the web."

"Dai Bach is a local man down the way who does a bit of building now and again," the red-headed Cerys volunteered from the corner. "He redid our kitchen for us, so he did, but you won't get him to work on that mill for love nor money."

"Well, a handyman, then?" John asked. "We've got one coming to help set up the beds this afternoon, but he had to come from the next town over. It might be helpful to have one more local. We're sure to have a lot of work for him."

His grin was still broad, but Abbie thought there was just a touch of desperation in his voice now.

The locals looked at each other but didn't speak.

John ran a hand through his hair. It had kept the thickness she had always admired in it, though it was greying at the temples now. "I just need a hand.

I don't think Abbie and I can disconnect the wheel on our own, that's all."

And there it was again—that strange shift in the air, as if the atmosphere had altered slightly. The other patrons were definitely eyeing each other up again now.

"Disconnect the wheel?" Mari leant forwards, resting her plump elbows on the counter. Her eyes were exceptionally shrewd as they pinioned them in place. "What's that now?"

"The waterwheel of the mill. It was creaking round and round all night. Could barely get a lick of sleep. I'm sure we'll all get used to it in time, but I thought it might be easier just to have it secured in place and disconnected from the water race."

Mr Edwards coughed and opened his mouth, but Mari just glared at him. "Don't," she said sharply. "Just leave it alone now, you hear? Come on, you lot. Eat up and get out. I've got to clear the tables for the next customers."

Abbie looked down at her own plate. She'd barely made a dent in it, but her stomach was swirling too much for food now. She laid her cutlery down. "We should get going too," she said. "We've got so much to do today."

John was about to protest, but she gave him a

look and he just grimaced instead. "Come on then, kiddos, you heard your mum. Finish up quickly now."

He matched the action to the words, cramming the last of his sausages in his mouth and washing it down with the tea, before pushing his chair back and getting to his feet.

Abbie thought she might feel a bit better outside the stuffy air of the café, but though the brisk autumnal breezes swirled around her, they couldn't sweep away the unease spreading, tumour-like, through her stomach. Her muscles were beginning to ache, for she didn't think she'd relaxed once since they'd first driven through the gate with their moving van and family car yesterday lunchtime.

She flinched as footsteps echoed behind them and she couldn't quite have said why. London was surely far more dangerous than this little retirement village, and yet she found her hands bunching into fists as she turned, as if ready to defend herself. But it was only Mr Edwards rushing after them, looking far more spritely than a man his age ought to. His withered hand seized Abbie around the wrist with surprising strength. She veered away instinctively but couldn't pull himself out of her grasp.

"Hey!" John said, outraged, but Abbie couldn't

say a word. Her eyes were fixed on his, frozen in place.

"You've got two beautiful kids there, *cariad bach*," Mr Edwards said. "Don't let them near the millpond. Your daughter, in particular."

"They know how to swim," John said again, crossly, just as he had last night. He seized Mr Edward's hand and flung it off Abbie's wrist, glowering at the old man. Abbie still stood there, as lifeless as one of her own sculptures. She could still feel the phantom pressure of his fingers manacling her wrist, as if she was chained here, locked in the path before her already.

"Swimming won't help," Mr Edwards said starkly. "It's very deep and very old. Accidents happen there. Well, folks call them accidents..."

The car crash. It's already begun.

The memory of last night was already blurring around the edges, until she couldn't be sure what she had really seen and what was just the figment of her imagination. She had been so certain at the time that there had been a shadow there, long hair, malevolent eyes. It wasn't an owl, whatever John said, but it could, conceivably, have been a shadow from one of the nearby trees, swaying in the moonlight.

But it seemed so solid. So real.

Her chest began to seize up, the remnants of old nightmares clenching across her ribcage. She twitched as if she was wrenching at the steering wheel once more. She didn't even know why she had headed that way. It would have made far more sense to swerve in the other direction, but it was as if some irresistible gravity had drawn her, magnet-like, towards those depths.

Don't overthink it now. It was just an instinctive flinch.

"We're going to put up a fence," she whispered.

He grimaced. "Well, that might help, perhaps," but he didn't sound as if he believed it, and his watery eyes still silently implored her.

"We've got to go, Mr Edwards," John said loudly. "The handyman will be here soon, and we have a lot of unpacking to do."

Mr Edwards nodded uneasily, but his eyes still didn't leave Abbie's.

"Take care of them," he mouthed at her as John tugged her away. "Be safe."

And those words echoed in her head with every hurried footstep home.

. . .

Abbie half expected the house to be burnt down by the time they'd wandered their way back to it again, but it sat in sturdy, waiting silence, just as it had when they left. As they scurried back through the front door, Abbie found herself ducking her head and holding her breath—refusing to glance towards the pond as if, foolishly, that might make it notice her somehow.

She let out all her breath at once in one large *whoosh* when John finally closed the front door behind them all, though.

"Right," he said. "You, kids, finish unpacking your rooms. I'll unpack the kitchen and the bathroom. Abs, what are you going to do? The studio? The living room?"

"No. I'm going to scrub the whole house with bleach, top to bottom," she said firmly. "It's not good to breathe in mould, and this place is covered in it. And whilst I'm doing that, I'm going to make a running list of all the fixtures that need replacing. Half the tiles in the bathroom are missing, and the skirting board in the kitchen is riddled with damp. That whole thing will need replacing."

"Alright. Sounds good." John clapped his hands together cheerily. "Come on, team, let's see how much we can do by lunchtime!"

Sophie rolled her eyes with an audible *urgh,* and Max barely seemed to have heard at all, still buried in his book, but Abbie gave her husband a bright smile. John, at least, was a reliable source of sunshine, even in these dark days.

By the time that John came to tell her that the handyman had arrived and the children were asking when lunch was, Abbie's arms were aching so much she could barely lift them. Her old pinafore dress, which she usually used as an art apron, was speckled with so much bleach that you could barely tell what the original colour had been, and she thought she'd never get the pungent scent of it all out of her skin. But slowly, patiently she was beating back the years of mould and neglect to a habitable state once more.

John perched on one of the still-taped up boxes as he chatted to her.

"The handyman seems nice," he said. "More friendly than the locals in the café, anyway. Less given to dire warnings of terrible fates." He rolled his eyes companionably. "He's up there now, starting on the kids' beds. He said it shouldn't take him too long, an hour or two to get them all up, he reckons. I'm going to ask him if he'll look at that wheel with me, too. If the bed is up and the wheel is silent, I might get a good night's sleep tonight."

He grinned at her, wearily.

Abbie frowned at him. "Did you really hear that wheel going last night?"

"Of course! Couldn't you? It was loud enough to wake the dead! I swear, Abs, you could sleep through anything." He laughed that wonderful, reassuring laugh of his, threading his arms around her waist and pulling her down onto his lap. "At least one of us is well rested today, I suppose."

But Abbie hadn't *been* asleep. In fact, she had been lying awake beside John, listening to him grunting, snuffling and snoring, the adrenaline of her near-miss car crash and the growing wordless dread she couldn't shift not releasing her enough to rest. She had heard the call of the birds outside, the distant yowl of an unhappy cat, and the rustle of the wind in the woods that surrounded them.

She hadn't heard the wheel go round, even once.

He must have dreamed it.

"Before you ask about the waterwheel, ask about a fence around the millpond," she said. "That's the next, most important job."

John groaned. "The kids are smart enough not to fall in, Abs, I really think—"

"You promised," she reminded him firmly. "And if that handyman is as efficient as you think he is, perhaps he will have time to do both."

John huffed, but agreed, so she pressed a kiss to his cheek. "I'll make a cuppa for you to take up to the handyman and then get on with those lunches," she said, peeling off her rubber gloves and throwing them to the floor. "Remember, the fence!"

She wisely pretended she did *not* hear the muttered reply as he stumped away.

After a hasty lunch and a catch up with the kids, she took herself back off to the studio room to finish scrubbing up. She was almost finished now, she thought, which was just as well because she was just about ready to drop. She stood back to admire her handiwork, staring around the room. The inner workings of the water wheel—a thick, rusty, cog spiked inner wheel within the room here—clung to the far wall. A conversation piece, John had called it. It looked like it was rusted firmly to the wall and she would have been willing to bet it couldn't have moved for love nor money...

And yet John said that he had heard it go...?

She almost startled out of her skin as the door slammed open behind her.

"Pah! You can't get good help these days," John

grumbled, barging his way into the room. "Always slacking off."

Abbie laughed. "Me? I've hardly been slacking! I've been here scrubbing away the mould since lunchtime. I don't want to speak too soon, but I think I might be done." She gestured towards the gleaming window seals, now back to a fresh, if somewhat old, off-white colour. They would probably need replacing anyway, but at least they wouldn't be breathing in anything unsavoury in the meantime.

"I wasn't talking about you, Abs. It's that handyman. He's only gone and dumped the fence panels by the pond and scarpered."

Abbie's smile fell at once. She tried to speak, but her throat had constricted so tightly she felt like she could barely breathe.

I thought we were going to be safe. I thought it was going to be alright.

"I'm going to phone him. He can't just ditch stuff like that," John said, pacing the floor, fuming. "That wood was expensive. It could have got damaged just lying around like that."

Why would he leave? We hadn't even paid him for the beds yet. He was meant to leave us an invoice. What on earth could have made him flee like that?

She stared distantly at John, who was talking fiercely down the phone now, but she could barely hear what he was saying though he was only a few feet away.

What if the handyman saw the same strange shadow by the pond that I saw last night? What if it tried to draw him in too? What if it was all real?

"Yeah, mate, and to you," John snapped, hanging up fiercely.

Abbie glanced over at him.

"The gall of that man!" John ranted, still stalking the empty room. "He had the temerity to say that you had told him not to do it!"

"Not to do what?"

"Put the fence up! Said he was just digging the last stuff out of the van when you started yelling at him from behind the curtains in the window to go away and that you'd changed your mind!"

She gaped at him, incredulously. "What? I was the one who wanted the fence up in the first place!"

"That's what I told him! I said if he was going to make excuses, he could at least make believable ones! Said you were quite rude to him too, so he just shoved the wood out of the van and drove off in a huff. He's not coming back, he said. We can just find another handyman or do it ourselves! Said he'll email the invoice through. Ha!"

"Why would I yell from the window?" She asked perplexed. "And we haven't even got the curtains up yet!"

"That's exactly what I said. He said he knows what he saw—a dark shadow twitching in the window, yelling at him. He said, he assumed it was curtains, but it could have been a blanket or something if we're going to be finicky about it. Then he said a lot more stuff, most of which was unrepeatable and hung up on me."

Abbie put her hands to her mouth. They wouldn't stay still, trembling there against her lips.

A shadow. He saw a shadow. Inside *the house. Here! Where we are!*

"Hey now, don't look like that. I'm no stranger to hard work. I can get that fence up all on my lonesome." John pulled her into a hug and winced. "Gah, you're freezing! Go and put a jumper on, love."

But Abbie didn't feel cold at all. She felt strangely warm, as if the cold all around her couldn't touch her now.

Running a fever maybe. Coming down with something.

But her thoughts sat fractured and disjointed in her mind.

A sudden wave of fear overtook her, swallowing all other thoughts whole. "The children! Where are the children?"

"I suspect Abbie's still in her bedroom unpacking, and Max was heading off to play in the garden last I saw."

Panic fizzed and crackled like tv static in her mind, until she couldn't even hear her own thoughts. Yelping wordlessly, she fled for the outdoors.

The afternoon sunlight was dying now. It sent long shadows stretching all around them, tree-branch limbs striping prison bars across the floor in rows of light and shade. The chill of the woods shuddered over her skin. He wasn't in the front yard, not by the family car, not by the piled-up wood, not by the gate at the top of the hill, nor by the thickly berried yew bushes that hemmed them all in like prison fences.

She turned slowly towards the mill pond.

Max was on the far side of the water. Alive! Still alive! She forced her limbs forwards, lurching towards him, screaming his name. The sound was oddly muted by the millpond, as if the waters were snatching it away somehow. Fear clawed its way up her throat, burning hot.

"Max! Max! Get away from the water!"

The words resonated back at her, whispering on the winds, strangely altered, it seemed, by the reverberations of the woods hemming them in.

Get away. Water.

He didn't hear her, still balancing along a log, teeteringly close to the water's edge.

"Max! Get inside!"

Inside. Hide.

She cursed beneath her breath. "Wait, I'll come to you."

Come for you. Coming for you.

She almost wept as the echoes slipped sinuously through the air, but she sprinted her way around the edge of the murky pool, all but flying.

Max wobbled, throwing his arms out wildly to regain his balance.

Her heartbeat echoed her pounding footsteps, until all she could hear was the rush of blood in her ears and the taste of fear dancing along her tongue.

"Max!"

He turned, right on the waters' edge. She hauled him into her arms, tugging them both away from the pond.

"Get off, Mum!" He struggled out of her arms with an impatient frown. He'd never really liked physical contact much. "What's the matter?"

She could have shaken him. Instead, she pulled him into another tight hug, her fingers becoming claws in his shirt.

"Don't go near the water! Don't you know how dangerous it is?"

"I wasn't doing anything! Why are you so cross?"

John panted up behind her in a lolloping sort of half-jog. He was looking at her strangely, and she knew she must seem half-mad, but she couldn't care now. The adrenaline was still pounding too fiercely in her veins.

"You're alright, aren't you, kiddo?" he said, gently pulling Max free from her viper embrace. "No harm, no foul. Your mum's just a bit worried you'll fall into the pond. It might be best to stay away from it for now, alright?"

"I was only looking for you, Mum," Max said.

She gaped at him. "Me? Why were you looking for me out here?"

"I heard your voice. I thought you'd come out to find me, but I couldn't see you anywhere. It seemed to be coming from over here though, so I just kept searching. It was loudest by the pond."

They all turned to stare at the murky black waters. It rippled back at them. Tauntingly, it seemed to Abbie.

John slung his arm over Abbie's shoulder, grinning at his son. "You know what it is? It's the acoustics in that mill room, I reckon. Your mum was just there, on the other side of that wall, all the time you were looking for her." He gestured to the large wheel and the thick stone wall behind it. "There must be a hole somewhere there, for spoking the wheel or something, and the sound carries through the hole, out over the water and echoes here." He hit his forehead suddenly, his eyes going wide. "That must be what happened earlier! You were cursing the mould you were busy trying to scrub away, Abs, the handyman heard you effing and blinding, thought you were talking to him, took umbrage and left in a huff."

Abbie chewed her lip. Her eyes drifted to the waters again. They were dancing, the last of the sunlight glinting off the softly swirling surface.

"What about the shadow in the sitting room window?" she whispered. "I wasn't even in that room. I was around the side of the house."

"Well, he had to say something, didn't he?" John said bracingly. "Couldn't admit he was hearing disembodied voices. Come on. You go inside and have a nice cup of tea. I'll get started with this fence, eh? Then you can stop worrying."

All of them turned towards the water, as if it was calling their name.

Something swirled with a slow, deliberate malevolence across the rippling surface of the lake then, heading towards them. It was white, and Abbie couldn't even begin to guess what it was. For a moment, she thought it looked a little like a cloth, or one of those old white, frilled caps folks used to wear in the old days.

"Don't, John!" She clutched at his arm as he reached for it curiously, but he shook her off.

"You've got to get a hold of yourself, Abs," he told her in an undertone, more fiercely than he usually did. "This is becoming a monomania for you." He bent down and fished it out of the waters, shaking the drips off. "There, you see, it's just the newspaper from the fish and chips I chucked in the pond this morning. Serves me right for littering, I suppose. Come on. Let's go in. We've still got half the rooms to unpack."

He thrust the dripping paper into Abbie's hands,

and she stared down at it. The ink had smeared and run, the picture of the placard wielding, glowering parents was unrecognisable now, the story confined to illegible history. Only three words remained unsullied at all, it seemed.

No justice. Innocent.

Abbie dropped the paper with a yelp and scurried after John and Max. She couldn't shake the feeling that the pond was watching her, all the way around.

CHAPTER 3
THE FORGOTTEN ROOM

John had always rather liked mornings, even on cold and cloudy ones like these, when he hadn't slept all that well the night before. They always felt like fresh beginnings, somehow. One more chance to right the mistakes of yesterday and take another step towards your goals. Abs had always cursed his somewhat cheery morning disposition, so he tried to keep it at least moderately in check in deference to her feelings, but today, somehow, he just couldn't help it. He felt *good*.

"It's nice to wake up in a proper bed again. I don't like to think I'm getting old, but sleeping on the floor certainly makes me feel it now." John stretched and grinned over at Abbie. She didn't say anything, just gave him a small, silent smile. She didn't snuggle up closer to him as she usually did, but lay there, perfectly still, and pallid.

He frowned at her. "You look a little peaky. Are you feeling alright?"

"Yes. I just didn't sleep well." Her voice was odd, somehow, though he couldn't have put his finger on why for the life of him.

"Because of that damned waterwheel, I'll be bound." The soft creak and splash of it had been incessant all through the night once again. It was odd, he never noticed it during the day—perhaps because it was nosier, or they were too busy to notice—but all night long the sound had echoed around their new bedroom, until it had even begun invading his dreams, chasing him through his sleep with its inevitable screech and scrape. He scratched his fingers over the stubble on his chin with a small, uneasy laugh, and grinned over at her. "Whose silly idea was it to buy a converted mill anyway?"

But Abbie didn't laugh back. She didn't even smile this time. His stomach lurched. He'd never seen her like this before.

Maybe she didn't really want to move, but she didn't feel like she could tell me. Maybe this is her way of saying something now...

But that wasn't like Abbie either. She had never really had secrets from him before.

He shuffled closer to her in the bed and pulled her up against his chest. She didn't resist, but she didn't snuggle in closer either. Utterly passive and hollow.

"Did you have a nightmare?" he asked gently. "It wouldn't be surprising, in the circumstances. You're under a lot of pressure."

She hesitated.

"You can tell me," he murmured, "we're a team."

"You already think I'm paranoid."

"No, I don't!" he lied immediately. "I want to support you."

She peeled herself out of his arms and shuffled her way to the edge of the bed so that her back was to him. As she perched on the end of the mattress, she buried her head in her hands. "I don't really remember it." The words were muffled and John had to strain to catch them. "They were just sharp fragments, disjointed images that made no sense. Dead cats and old books, broken glass and screaming."

He rubbed a hand down her back. "That sounds awful. It's just a nightmare though, Abs. It can't hurt you."

"I know," she snapped. And, again, that was

unlike her. She wasn't given to losing her temper usually. She got to her feet without looking at him. "I'm getting in the shower. You sorted out the boiler?"

"I think so. You'll soon find out," he teased weakly.

She didn't reply at all, just drifted away, spectral and vague, leaving him alone.

For a moment, John could do nothing but stare at the doorway she'd glided through.

A sudden surge of decisiveness swept over him. He couldn't just sit around doing nothing. That wouldn't solve anything at all. He would throw some clothes on and finish that fence he'd started yesterday afternoon. Once it was completed, Abbie would calm down again, and things could go back to normal.

He had slipped into his jeans scarcely before he'd finished thinking, and was already halfway out the front door as he hauled his jumper over his head.

Damn, but it was brisk out here today. It had been a mild autumn so far, but it was freezing down in this dip. The dew had crystalised, frosting the leaf mould, kissing the last leaves clinging onto the trees and dusting the yew berries until they looked like sugary treats.

Still, a bit of hard graft this morning will soon warm me up.

But he cursed out loud as he turned to his work. All the fence panels he had put up last night had immediately fallen down again, scattering like chaff through the surrounding mud.

He growled low under his breath. *I must not have driven them in deeply enough.*

It was hard to dig here. The topsoil was damp and claggy, clay-like around the waters, but beneath were lots of roots and rocks, making it difficult to get a solid purchase on it. The prudent thing to do would be to get some sort of small digger in, but that would all be extra money, wouldn't it?

And time. They'd never come today, and then Abbie will have another night of paranoia. I'll just have to do the best I can.

He was sweating like a pig before he'd even got the fence panels secured halfway around the pond, but he persevered, even when his muscles began to scream at him, and the chill autumn winds turned his damp back icy.

The surface of the pond seemed to ripple with every swing and thud of his hammer, driving the poles deep into the earth, hemming it in. The rhythmic thud and clunk of it ought, surely, to echo across those swirling waters, but it was oddly quiet. Only a distant, disembodied woman's voice called to him from the surface of the water, mingling with a soft feline yowl of displeasure.

He stopped for a moment, clinging onto the last fence post with his blistered fingers. He couldn't quite make out the words, muffled as they were, drifting across the surface of the pool like a morning mist.

"Abbie must be back in the mill room again, talking to herself," he said, aloud. Though where that damned cat was, he still didn't know. It must have got trapped in a tree hollow somewhere or locked in a shed or something. It was about time someone did something about it.

And yet he couldn't help but notice that his own voice didn't seem to echo across the water as Abbie's did. He shivered slightly. "Strange things, acoustics."

Still, he drove the last of the fence panels into the soil with a great thud and stepped back to admire his work.

Well, it wasn't exactly *straight,* that was for certain. In fact, looking at it now, it seemed that each of the fence posts pointed in an entirely different direction. They pointed, jagged and sharp, all around the pond find in a ragged circle, like crooked teeth. Yes, there was something decidedly canine and predatory about them, as if they guarded the gaping, hungry maw within, ready to devour them all.

He laughed to himself uneasily. "I'm not sure Abs will like it. If anything, I've made it look even more dangerous. Maybe we should start selling tickets to the *mystic mill pond*. We might make a bit of money to open our gallery properly."

There was no one there to appreciate this fine bit of humour, so John took himself inside to find the others. And he certainly didn't walk any quicker than he usually did or feel the malevolent stare of the pond leering up behind him, prickling at the back of his neck, for that would be ridiculous.

He found Abbie back in the mill room, staring up at the ceiling again.

"Abs?"

She startled around, her face instantly paling. She tried to replace it with a smile, but it was too late, he had already seen it.

"What's the matter?"

"It's nothing. It doesn't matter."

But her eyes drifted up to the ceiling again. He glanced up too. The mould was back.

Already?

"I thought you'd cleaned that all away yesterday?" He frowned.

"So did I, but apparently not." She gave an unconvincing laugh and tugged him away towards the centre of the room, away from the grey shadow creeping across the plasterwork. "You wanted me?"

"Just got the fence up."

Relief, pure and sweet, seeped across her face. She smiled, and, for half a moment, she looked just as young and carefree as when he had first met her. He pulled her into his arms. It had all been worth it then, the early morning and the aching limbs, the sweat and the blisters and the bitter autumn winds. He kissed her.

"Thank you, John. I know you think I'm silly"

"Cautious," he corrected her. "A wonderfully cautious realist. Which balances out my eternal optimism rather nicely, don't you think?"

She chewed her lip, staring up at him with watering eyes. "I'm *sure* I saw something, John. It felt so *real*. Something dangerous, that doesn't *want* us here."

She rested her head against his chest with a soft breath.

Surreptitiously, he pulled the phone from his pocket and pulled up the search engine.

Can breathing in mould make you crazy? He typed, and then, because that felt vaguely disloyal, he rephrased it to *make you paranoid?*

The circle whirled on the screen for a few moments and then an error message popped up to say there was no internet available.

Damn it. I forgot to order the wi-fi extender when we were in the village yesterday.

He closed the tab quickly, before Abbie could see.

"Why don't you take the kids into the big town over the way?" he said hastily. "It's only about half an hour away. It's bound to have more shops and things. They can choose new posters and lampshades for their room, choose what colour they want to paint it, all that sort of thing. It will keep them out of trouble while I'm working. Besides, you need a break. And I've got a list the length of my arm of things we need to pick up."

She peeled herself away from him and wiped her face. "That's a good idea. I'd like to get away from it all for a bit. And the kid's will be starting their new schools soon. We should make the most of them whilst they're here. I think we're *technically* supposed to be homeschooling them in the interim..."

"Life is an education," John said briskly.

"Besides, I was never much good at sitting through school. I was always far better at, what do they call it now, self-directed learning? I reckon the kids are the same. Aren't you?" he asked loudly as Max wandered past the studio door towards the kitchen, hunting out a snack.

Max poked his head through the studio doorway, then his eyes went gleefully wide. "Hey, Mum! Look! It looks like there's a person on the ceiling behind you!"

Abbie froze.

John glanced up too and chortled. "Yeah, if you sort of squint a bit, those mould marks do look a bit like someone's shadow. Well, if you're imaginative enough, anyway. I'm afraid your new friend will be leaving soon though, because your mum's going to buy extra strength bleach from town. Go and fetch your coat and your sister. You'll be going in with her too, alright?"

Max scampered away. Abbie gave John a strained smile.

John's heart sank. So much for her new-found relief.

All it takes is one misplaced comment and she's back to this doubting waif again?

"You're sure you're alright?" John murmured,

catching her hand. "Damn, Abs, you'd best get some gloves whilst you're there. Your fingers are icicles."

Normally, she'd retaliate by squirreling them under his top and pressing them against his stomach, stealing his warmth. Today she just gave him that same, silent smile he didn't believe and just drifted away.

He fought the urge to curse and shout. He and Abs had *always* been on the same team before. They'd faced challenges, of course, but they'd always faced them together. He couldn't remember ever feeling so *isolated* from her before. How could one little house be the thing that broke apart their rock-solid marriage?

Or were there always cracks in our relationship? Cracks I just didn't notice, or didn't want to see...

For a moment, he thought about going after her. Maybe the two of them could do with a day away from it all. They could go to town with the kids, grab a coffee, maybe some lunch, browse the shops...

But all this work is still going to be here when we get back. It would be better to just get it all finished, and then we can relax properly once it's all done.

He scrubbed a hand over his eyes, fighting the exhaustion building there as the front door slammed and the distant roar of an engine carried his family away.

"Come on, what are we going to do next? Pick a nice job, John, then it won't feel so much like work," he advised himself with a grin. He rubbed his hands together, scanning through the room.

He'd measure the back wall for windows, that's what he'd do. Then he could mark it off with some masking tape, and he'd know how much of the rest of the wall he had spare for shelves and cupboards and the like. If he could get those attached today, they could unpack half the boxes in this room and they'd be near enough done.

Whistling, he dug out his trusty measuring tape and a roll of masking tape. That small smear of Sophie's blood was still there across the wall, he noticed. He went to get a cloth and some bleach to clean it away, but as he put out a hand to steady himself against the back wall, he frowned. It felt far warmer than the other, thick cold stone walls around here, and it shifted slightly beneath his touch, as if it was loose. He rapped a knuckle on it.

A stud wall? But the surveyor's report hadn't shown that?

The distant hissing of the cat sounded again, angry and frightened. It couldn't, surely, have locked itself behind the *wall?* It would be long dead by now if it had?

Unless there's a hole from the outside. The poor beast must have squeezed its way into the from the outside and can't get out again. No wonder it's been so frantic lately! No wonder we've been able to hear it but can't see it anywhere!

Well, it would be his good deed for the day to rescue it then, wouldn't it?

He reached for his hammer and, with a somewhat gleeful smile, took a massive swing at the wall. It probably wasn't a good DIY technique and Abs certainly would have had a thing or two to say about it if she was still here but it certainly felt cathartic to engage in a bit of mindless destruction now.

Splinters, plaster and old paint chips came spitting out of the wall with each hammer blow, but John didn't stop. He threw his whole weight behind it, all the frustration and anger, the anxiety, the exhaustion, the constant strain of always having to be the cheerful one, the rock who never wavered, the voice of reason—until the hammer fell all the way through and a great chunk of wall cascaded to his feet.

There seemed to be a small room trapped

beyond, but there was no sign of a yowling moggy at all. In fact, nothing living seemed to be within.

Darkness swam out of the hole to greet him, impenetrable and sinister. The air was musty-thick, as if it hadn't been disturbed for hundreds of years, John thought fancifully.

"Now I know how those archaeologists felt discovering King Tut's tomb," he joked aloud, though there was no one there to hear it, as if the sound of his voice might dispel the prickling unease stuttering across his spine. If anything, it made it worse. The false note lingering there was far too obvious.

He licked his lips. "Well, I've started now. I might as well carry on."

Fighting the growing feeling that he was about to pull the whole house down upon his head, he donned some old gardening gloves and began ripping out the old timber planks of the stud wall by hand. These were no new MDF sheets. These were old, rotting timbers. They crumbled damply in his hands as he tugged at them. This little nook hadn't been boarded over by the last developers, that was clear enough.

There are secrets here, squirreled away for centuries.

He felt quite privileged to be the one to unearth them.

He pulled another chunk free and it crumbled into a hole large enough to squeeze through. He almost ran then, but his curiosity had always been stronger than his survival instincts. Turning on the torch on his phone, he edged his way inside.

He stood in the centre of the cramped little hiding room and swivelled slowly, the torch scanning round the blackness like a lighthouse beam. Wild stories were already forming in his eager mind. Maybe this was one of those—what did you call them? Priest holes? —from the days of the catholic persecutions. What era was that now? Max would know. Or maybe some previous owner had built it as an emergency hideaway in case the violence of the French Revolution seeped across to British shores. He vaguely remembered something about that from school.

Or we are in Wales—maybe they built it to hide from the English! Wouldn't that be an irony, since we were the ones who found it? Ha!

A thrill of excitement was building in him irresistibly. This was history, here! Real, living history! And he owned a part of it! All his growing uneasiness about Abbie and this whole move was washed away with the thrill of it.

Without realising it, he began to pace the narrow space, his thoughts already whirling. They'd have to do some proper research, of course. Maybe contact a local historian... but this could be what their first exhibition was about! A nice local topic, get the neighbours back on board. Yes, they'd have little historical fact-boards and snippets and things up alongside the paintings and sculptures. Maybe they could even make a play on the name for the gallery, call it *Hidden Gems,* or some such thing. He'd have to think about it. And—

—something skittered away from his foot. He yelped, startling, swishing the phone light down to the floor immediately. He expected to see a mouse fleeing, but no. A small leather journal lay half-tumbled across the floor. He must have accidentally kicked it as he paced. He knelt, barely daring to breathe. His fingers brushed the leather, which was peeling in places, but seemed to have escaped the damp cavorting around the rest of the house. Beside it, a strange fabric-wrapped bundle sat, the stiff leather holding a distinctly mildewy smell as he fumbled it open one handed. An array of old, rusted tools glinted in the torch light. An old knife, a small pestle, a small round stone with a hole in the middle, which looked a little like one of those large millstones, except it was about a thousand times smaller.

Miller's tools from the original mill? But this place hasn't been a working mill since before the industrial revolution, the estate agents said.

His heart jolted. He'd hoped this little tucked away room was an old find, but this was even better than he'd dreamed. This old treasure trove must have been from right back when the mill was first made. An original addition.

He licked his lips and scanned his torch around the room again, hoping for even more treasures. He was in luck. In the very far corner, there was another shadowy lump which must be another parcel, and there, a small old mirror was propped up against the wall. He crept towards it, scarcely able to believe his luck. It was blackened with age and shattered into a thousand shards, which clung together with a stubborn perseverance he could scarcely credit—surely, in the past, four hundred odd years, they ought to have fallen? The wall behind the mirror had deep scratch marks carved into it, but they were not in any words John recognised.

John tilted his head to one side, thinking hard.

There was a puzzle in this. He was even starting to believe it was all just an elaborate hoax. Weren't mirrors supposed to be ridiculously expensive in the 1600s? Even small ones like this. So, what was it doing here?

Perhaps that is why they kept it, even though it was broken? And perhaps that was why they locked it away, to protect it.

He glanced at the unopened journal. Surely a book would have been costly too. And didn't Max say something once about the high levels of illiteracy before the Victorians made schooling compulsory? Would the miller in a small rural Welsh village even be able to read?

Unless he only kept it for its monetary value. Perhaps this is what this room is, a bank vault, of sorts. Or where the miller kept his stolen loot, of course, he added with a grin to himself.

He could just see the whole sordid tale now; a miller by day, a highway man by night, scurrying his loot into the depths of the mill until he could sell it on.

Ha! I could make a dozen different paintings about that!

"Mustn't get ahead of myself," he muttered, but

THE WATER MILL

the grin was still firmly plastered onto his face. He reached for the second parcel, half hoping to find some famously missing jewels, or a coronet or something there.

But as he peeled the fabric back, his hand brushed against something *furry*.

He leapt back with a yelp, dropping the phone. The torchlight illuminated the cloudy eyed stare of a black, mummified cat, stiff and dusty.

The cat sounds...

But that was ridiculous. This cat had clearly been dead for years, decades, even, from the state of it. It couldn't be making noises now...

"It wasn't a cat hissing and spitting at all, I bet," he said aloud, rather unconvincingly. "You know what it was, it was the gas hissing in the pipes. That's all."

Which didn't explain the yowling, or how he could hear it outside, of course, but he was not going to let his imagination run away with him now.

John looked back down at the cat again, still half wrapped in its cloth. It just made *no* sense! Why would anybody keep a dead cat? Unless it had wandered in by mistake, been trapped when the walls were raised, and then died? But it was wrapped in the fabric? That seemed deliberate, as if it had been a beloved pet, as if someone regretted its death and wanted to bury it properly…

A shadow fell across the torch light, casting him into gloom. He turned to see Abbie standing there in the threshold he had hacked away. He flinched. He hadn't realised how long he had been busy tearing down the walls and poking around in here. It had seemed only minutes, as if time was frozen in here somehow, but if she had returned already, it must have been hours.

"Hey, Abs. Look what I've found!" he started enthusiastically, but she dropped the carrier bags in her hands, her eyes fixed on the cat.

She screamed.

The scream seemed to shatter the small bubble of excitement that had permeated the little nook, turning it at once from an exciting treasure trove into a place of danger and fear.

Still screaming madly, she ran for the door. He sprinted after her, bursting out of that tiny little room back into the warm embrace of reality instead.

"Abbie, wait!" He caught her, but she thrashed like a wild animal, caught in a snare.

"Let me go! We have to leave! We're in danger! The kids!"

He gaped at her, trying to hold her still. "Leave? Where? What are you talking about?"

She collapsed against his chest, weeping hysterically. "The cat! The shadow! The crash!"

He grabbed onto the first words, because they were the only ones that made sense to him right now. "So, because some poor cat got stuck in an old, disused room and died, the children are in danger? Is that what you're saying?"

She shoved him away, veering from fear to anger to reckless paranoia with dizzying haste. Her eyes were wide and rabbit-like, darting around the room constantly, as if she could see some fresh danger creeping up on them even now. He stared at her, helplessly.

"That cat was in my dream! I saw it before it happened! How do you explain that?"

"You said you didn't really remember your dream this morning," he pointed out. "Why are you so certain the cats are the same? Just because you dreamed about *a* cat, doesn't mean..."

But she wasn't listening. "It's an omen! And the car crash, the disembodied voices! There's something supernatural here and if we don't leave now, it will kill us! Phone the estate agent, we're putting it back on the market!"

Supernatural.

Abbie had always delighted in creating supernatural sculptures, creating something impossible and making it look so very plausibly real, but he'd never once thought she actually believed any of that stuff.

"Abbie," he began, but she had already begun to wrestle his phone out of his jeans pocket, searching for the number he'd saved there. Her hands trembled as she dialled it. "This was our dream, Abs. We're never going to get another shot at..."

"My dream is not to bury my children, John. I must protect them. Hello?" she added, turning away as the estate agent picked up.

John sighed and rubbed his hands over his eyes. So much for all his vision of a new gallery. That exciting new exhibition he had planned was already fading from his mind ruefully.

We were a team, he thought again, bitterness lining every syllable, watching as his wife practically shrieked at the estate agent down the phone. *When did we start pulling in opposite directions? The Abbie I married would never make such a large decision without discussing it with me. She'd never try to put the house back on the market without my consent. Something has changed in her.*

He eyed the hole behind him wistfully once more. Maybe he could take the artefacts there with him, when they left. He supposed he ought to donate them to a museum, really, but it would be good to get a bit more information on them first. He would loath to give them up so soon after he had found them.

"No. No!" He turned as Abbie sank to the floor, weeping.

"What is it?"

"They said it took seven years to sell last time, and they don't think they're best placed to sell it for us again so soon," she sobbed. "They don't think it will sell at all." She curled up into a ball, letting his phone skitter across the floor once more.

He picked it up, then crouched beside her, rubbing her back. "Maybe you need to talk to someone, Abs."

"You *do* think I'm mad!" She glared at him, wiping her blotchy cheeks. "I dreamed about the contents of that room before you even knew it was there. How do you explain that?" she demanded again.

He eyed the room behind him once more. Even he had to admit that it did seem odd.

"Well, we can't afford to rent and hold a mortgage at the same time," he said reasonably. "If the estate agents don't think we can sell it on again, then we don't have any choice but to stay here, do we?"

She wept harder than ever at that. "The children, if they die, I'll never forgive myself."

"Look," he said, pulling her into his arms. "Here's what we're going to do. We'll get a vicar or someone to come in and do an exorcism, purge all the bad energy or whatever right out of the place. Then it will be the same as any other home, won't it? No more nightmares. No more shadows."

"I don't think they actually do those anymore." She hiccoughed.

"Then we'll get some hippy woman to come and burn some sage or whatever and dispel the evil spirits and bad aura, alright? It's all going to be OK. Besides, I've got that fence up now, so that'll keep the kids away from the pond, won't it? That's what you're really worried about, isn't it?"

The look she gave him was one of pure terror, and the hands which clung suddenly to his shirts were claws. "The fence! I forgot you said you'd put that up already!"

He frowned at her. "So? You wanted me to, didn't you? I was only trying to make you happy."

Why is nothing that I do good enough anymore?

But her next words came out as barely more than a hoarse, terror-laden whisper. "Every single fence post has been knocked down, already. It's gone, John."

CHAPTER 4
DROWNING

John lingered in the threshold of the front door, raising a hand to greet Cerys, the bottle-dyed red-head from the café. She marched purposefully down the driveway, her carrier bag swinging in her hands. There was a look of grim determination on her face, as if she was single-handedly marching into a warzone, but she had come at short notice and John was grateful for that.

Abbie had taken the children over to the next town to stay in a hotel overnight. Two hundred quid, for one night. Money they could scarcely afford to throw away right now.

Not a lot for our children's lives, John, she had snapped at him when he had tried—not unreasonably, he thought to point this out. *If you don't want to come, then don't.*

So, he hadn't. He had stayed, alone, in the house they had chosen, bought and paid for together. The house that he had thought was going to be their family's future.

It had been the first night since they'd been married that they'd ever spent apart, actually—save for the night after Max had been born, and Abs had had to stay in hospital overnight for monitoring. Max had been a far more complicated birth than Sophie, all things told. Now that he came to think of it, last night had felt remarkably similar to then. The same wordless fears swirling through his stomach. The same jittery energy making him pace the empty house alone. The same flinching at the smallest sound, checking his phone a dozen times a minute to see if there was news.

Birth and death aren't so different, after all, are they?

"You sent for me?" Cerys said as she pulled to a stop before him, startling him out of his reflections.

He gave her a pallid grin. "Thanks for coming," he said, "Mari in the café said that you were known to dabble with the occult. Abbie has been so worried about this millpond of ours. She thought she saw a shadow there, and the voices carry across the waters from inside the house, which can make it feel a bit spooky. I thought maybe if you did some sort of, I don't know, aura cleansing or something, it would make her feel a bit more comfortable."

Cerys gave him a shrewd look. "You're a sceptic," she said. "You think your wife is making it all up."

He gave her a helpless shrug and a small smile. "I'm open to having my mind changed," he lied. "I just want us all to be happy here."

She started to retort and then stopped herself, her eyes snagging on his jacket pocket. "What's that you've got there now?" she asked sharply.

"Just a book," John said hastily, covering the bulging shape with his hand to hide it from view. He wasn't ready to share the journal with anyone yet.

It was *fascinating,* though, of course, he couldn't read it. He had spent all night locked away in that tiny nook he had discovered, drawn there by some instinct he couldn't quite have explained. He had run his hands over the tools and the mirror so many times he thought he had committed them to memory. He'd even stroked the cat once or twice, as if it might come purring back to life under his touch and unravel this whole mystery for him.

But it was the journal that called to him the

most. The writing was neat and painstaking, blots of ink speckling the page as if the writer had paused to think. The letters were carved deep into each page, as if the writer had pressed down hard which made him think it was someone who was fairly new to literacy. The children had both written like that when they had first learned to write.

And yet, though on the surface, it meant nothing, he could not put it down. There were secrets hidden here. He could feel them almost humming beneath his fingertips every time he stroked that old leather cover. And he was desperate to unravel them.

He coughed, aware that Cerys was looking at him oddly. "So, what have you brought to help then?"

She dumped her bag at her feet and pulled her hair back into a ponytail, eyeing the pond with dislike. "Salt, mostly, and sage to burn. I've got a few crystals that I'll place around the waters—selenite is the best for absorbing negative energies and tourmaline for its protective qualities—and some candles to burn." She glanced at the waters. It swirled darkly back at them. Cerys took a sharp breath, her jaw jutting out defiantly despite the fear in her eyes as she turned back to John. "But most of this stuff only works if you *believe*.

If you're bringing in your own bad energy and scepticism, I don't know that it's going to do much."

A wave of irritation crept over him. "Why did you come if you don't think you can help?"

She shrugged. "Your kids looked sweet, and I've got kids of my own. My boy Dafydd can't be much older than your eldest. I didn't want anything to happen to them. Your girl, in particular. We've found teenage girls are particularly susceptible to... accidents... around here. You need to keep an eye on her."

Thank goodness Abs wasn't here to hear that. She'd never step foot in the house again.

But John just gave her a small smile. "Alright. We'll try. I'll leave you to it, shall I? I don't want to disturb you."

She gave him a distant nod, still eyeing up the millpond with a curl-lipped glower. John crept away.

He told himself that he was going to finish unpacking the bathroom and fix the new blinds up over the window, not that they had any nosy neighbours who could peek through but, of course, he found himself back in that little nook again. The claustrophobic warmth enveloped him as he entered, as if capturing him and welcoming him home once more.

He ran his hands over the cracked glass of the mirror. He'd had the foresight to bring the large battery powered lantern in this time, and it illuminated the whole room, but still, shadows seemed to flicker over the shattered shards, leaping from one fragment to another in a strange, disjointed dance. He tried to follow the path of them, tried to work out whether, if he moved his arm like *this*, it would make the shadow move like *that,* but try as he might, he could not make his movements line up with the shadow's journey. It was almost as if the torchlight were trapped *within* the glass, shining right back out at him.

Fanciful nonsense. That's all.

But his skin prickled all the same.

The creak of the mill sounded louder than ever, as if it were closer somehow, accompanied by a quiet splash, incessant, persistent. Approaching.

And then, it was right behind him.

John whirled around with an oath. Cerys stood in the threshold, staring, wide-eyed around at the treasure trove.

Fool. It wasn't the creak of the waterwheel. It was

Cerys' footsteps on the floorboards. I'm getting just as bad as Abs.

He rubbed a hand over his chin. *The splash must just have been my imagination. Supplying the details.*

He almost believed it.

He got to his feet hastily. "Can I help you?"

"I'm done."

"What? Already?" he exclaimed, surprised. Clearly this mystic nonsense didn't take as long as he expected.

She gave him an odd look. "It's been over an hour now."

He blinked at that. It was this nook, that was what it was. It swallowed time somehow. It barely felt like he had squeezed through the hole in the wall five minutes ago.

"What is this place?" she added, looking around.

John tried to usher her away, oddly jealous of his newfound lair, but Cerys wouldn't be shifted. He laughed uneasily. "Are you going to tell me there is a bad aura here too?"

Slowly, Cerys shook her head. "There's no evil here," she said softly. "But there is fear. Desperation. Someone hid something here—something that they fervently needed and dared not be rid of, but which could kill them if it was found. I can feel the old traces of that desperate dread still lingering in the air. It cannot hurt you, but it makes me..." she struggled for the right word and finally alighted on, "sad. I wish I could have helped her."

"Her who?" John demanded. "I assumed this was the miller's hiding place."

Cerys bent to pick up the tools, gathering them in her arms in their leather cloth like a blanket-swaddled baby. "These are no millers' tools," she murmured gently. "These are the tools of witchcraft. That must have been why they were hidden. It would have been a death sentence, if they were found."

"So, it was bad magic haunting the pool, was it?" John asked, trying very hard to keep the sneer from his voice.

Again, Cerys hesitated. "I don't know," she confessed. "The aura there confused me. It was very muddled. There was a lot of push and pull at the same time. Like something was simultaneously trying to drag you in and shove you away. That's why it's so active here, I think. The magic is tangled. And it had a strong masculine aura," she added. "That's unusual. I don't know what to think."

John snatched the tools back from her, wrapping them carefully and replacing them near the mirror.

"Well, thanks all the same. How much do we owe you?"

But she just waved a dismissive hand at that. "We're neighbours now," she said. "And we want you to be safe. You can get me a bacon butty next time we're both in Mari's, if you really insist, and we'll call it even."

At least I haven't wasted any more money on this nonsense.

He smiled broadly and finally managed to usher her out of the room and back to the front door. "Abbie will be so relieved," he said. "I appreciate your time and help. Thanks."

"*Croeso,*" she retorted. "*Dim problem.* Any time." She caught at his wrist then. She was so short that she had to crane her neck up to meet his gaze, and it should have been comical but somehow, she was so utterly serious that it wasn't. "I mean that now, Mr Harper. Any time you need us, you call, you hear?"

And then she had gone before John had even worked out what to say next.

JOHN WENT AWKWARDLY BACK to the front door as he heard the rev of the engine chugging slowly down the driveway later that afternoon. He lingered in the threshold, holding up a hand in greeting to the kids, not really sure what to do next. They wouldn't meet his eyes.

The poor things are going to need therapy if this continues.

Not that they could afford that, if Abbie insisted on spending all their money on hotels, of course, but never mind. She'd come back when he called and told her that the aura had been cleansed. That was something. He was half expecting her never to return at all.

"Go and unpack your overnight bags," Abbie said curtly as she slammed the car door behind her. The sound echoed over the pool beside them, reverberating back with an angry clunk. The children gratefully scuttled away. John and Abbie stared at each other in the driveway for a long, uncomfortable moment. Then they both started speaking at once.

"Sorry, you go," John said, chuckling uneasily.

"I just... I know we left things badly last night. I didn't like arguing like that. It's not like us. We always work things out," Abbie said in a stilted way, not looking at him.

Is that supposed to be an apology?

But he supposed she didn't think she had

anything to apologise for. She was just trying to protect the children.

He rubbed his eyes. "I didn't like it either," he admitted. "Look, Abs, it's been a lot lately. Maybe we need to start making some more time for us. Go on a date again, or something. When was the last time we had a date night?"

"When could we find the time?" She gave a bitter, weary laugh that wrenched at his heart.

"We'll *make* the time." He slung his arms around her and pulled her up against his chest. Damn, she looked *exhausted,* as if she hadn't slept a wink, even in a comfortable hotel bed, far away from the creak and splash of the waterwheel and the pond that frightened her so much.

She stared up at him with big, blood-shot eyes. "We're alright, aren't we, John?"

"We're alright," he promised. "Always."

She rested her head on his chest, and he had to resist the sudden urge to sweep her up in his arms and carry her away, as if they were newlyweds.

I'd probably do my back in now though. We're neither of us as young as we once were.

"Tea?" he asked instead.

"Tea," she said decisively, threading her fingers through his.

. . .

SITTING in their new kitchen together, around the old, scuffed kitchen table, sharing a cuppa from their favourite mugs, it was almost as if nothing had ever changed, John thought. He filled her in on everything Cerys had said and done—except for the warning about Sophie. That would have been a step too far, he thought.

"She said it was a masculine aura?" Abbie said with a frown, cradling her mug. "But I..." she stopped, shaking her head. "Well, she's the expert, I suppose. I just want it all to be over now."

"Maybe you should get started on your next sculpture?" he suggested.

"Already? We haven't finished unpacking, or doing up the house, or getting the children settled in their new schools"

"I think it might help you," he said firmly. "You always work out your emotions through your art. Don't you think it might be good to have some sort of outlet for all the strain you've been under?"

She chewed her lip at that, and he could tell it sounded enticing. "I don't want to leave all the work to you..." she said uncertainly.

"I want to do it. Go on. Go and lock yourself in the studio and sketch out some ideas."

"Well, if you're *sure*..."

"Positive. I'll make sure the kids don't disturb you."

He was as good as his word, although, in truth, it didn't take much doing. Sophie had taken to locking herself in her bedroom of late, and when he went to check on Max, he found him curled up on the sofa in the living room, still reading that guidebook Abs had bought him.

"I don't think I've seen you take your nose out of that book all week," John teased. "What is so fascinating?"

Max held up the book so John could see the front cover. It seemed to be an old local area guide from the eighties or nineties, given the state of the cover and the lurid front illustration. "Mum found it in a charity shop for me before we moved. It's fascinating! Did you know that Anglesey used to be known as *Mam Cymru* during the Middle Ages? Because it was so fertile that it fed the rest of Wales, apparently. That's why there's so many mills here. They grew so much grain. It's also, famously, home of the village with the longest name in Wales." He took a deep breath and then, with a clearly practiced tongue said, "*Llanfairpwllgwyngyllgogerychwyrndrobwllllantysiliogogogoch.*" He gave John a triumphant, and somewhat smug, smile.

John obediently broke into applause. "That's certainly a mouthful! Just be glad we didn't move *there*. You'd never fit it all on one envelope!"

"It's not that far from here though. We could go and take a photo with the place sign, and then I could send it back to my old friends as a postcard, couldn't I?"

"It's a deal," John said, then he added, "You're pleased that we moved then?"

It would be a relief. One of us should be.

Max considered this for a moment, with that thoughtful way he always had. "Yes, I think so. As long as we don't meet any ghosts."

John's smile faltered. "You've been talking to your mum?"

"What? No. It was in the guidebook." He held it up to show John. "It said the villages around here also had a tragic past of witch-hunting. They even famously had a witch finder general come round these parts in the 17th century and had big trials and everything. According to legends, the spirits of the women he killed still linger in some places around here. I don't think I'd like to meet any ghosts, but especially not a witch's one," he said decisively. "And what if the Welsh from the old ages is different from the Welsh I'm learning? I wouldn't even be able to talk to it!"

John had to laugh at that. Max always thought of things that would never have occurred to him. "I wouldn't worry about it," he said. "They just put stuff like that in to sell the guidebooks, you know, make it sound more interesting and mysterious than it really is. Between you, me and the gatepost, I'm not sure that any of those women were really witches anyway. I think they were just some poor old souls who everyone picked on."

Max seemed to accept that, thankfully, and returned to his book without another word, so John slid off to the kitchen again to make a cuppa. He made one for Abbie too, and crept over to the studio holding it before him like a shield.

He placed it beside her on the table she was bent over, scrawling feverishly. Though she always told him off for peeking before she was ready, he peered over her shoulder to scan the sketches anyway. He gasped.

The scribbled, frenzied sketch was manic with repressed energy, as if it were about to come crawling right out of the page, snatching at the pen still scratching over it. There was the impression of hair, long, wet, dripping, and the hint of fabric in motion, a shawl or skirt or some such thing, but it was the two, large dark eyes fixed straight on the viewer that were the most disconcerting. He couldn't drop that black gaze, though it was only ink on paper. How Abbie had managed to capture such frightened, malevolent energy, he'd never know—nor how she would translate it to a real sculpture, creating the impression of motion without making it move—but if she pulled it off, it would be her greatest work to date. Of that, he was certain.

Not that anyone would actually want to buy that thing, of course. You wouldn't want it sitting in your back garden, after all. But I bet it would draw people out to the gallery. It could be the centrepiece of our opening exhibition. People would come from miles around to see it in person, I'm sure.

"That's amazing, Abs," he murmured, and she flinched with a yelp, almost sending the tea beside her flying.

She snatched the paper up to her chest protectively, but then slowly laid it back down again. She gave him a small, weak smile. "I didn't hear you come in."

"I'm not surprised. You were pretty absorbed in

your work." He picked up the sketch paper carefully. "We'll have to frame this and exhibit it alongside your sculpture in the new gallery, I reckon," he said. "You could even sell it separately, I think." He glanced down at her. "This is what your nightmares have been?"

She hesitated and then whispered; "The shadow I saw in the car. It looked like this."

He shuddered. "Well, no wonder you've been so on edge then!" He pressed a kiss to the top of her head. "I'm sorry. I probably could have been more supportive. I didn't realise it was as bad as all this."

She rubbed her eyes. "It's done now. I hope." Her eyes drifted to the sketch again. "I would have felt better if Cerys had seen the same thing I had though. That," she nodded at the picture, "does not seem like a masculine aura to me."

Cerys was making it up off the top of her head. But somehow John didn't think it would do any good to say that now.

"Would it have been better?" he snapped. "Or would it just have convinced you more than ever that you *did* see the shadow? That it wasn't just a dream?"

She startled, blinking over at him, and he couldn't blame her. He was caught a little by surprise by the sharpness of his tone too. He hadn't meant to be so angry about it all. He forced a quick smile to soften the words and, tentatively, she returned it.

"I don't know. Maybe you're right," she said. "We just need to put it all behind us now, I think."

"There you go! That's the spirit! Onwards and upwards, and all that." He pressed another kiss to her head, manically cheerful to make up for his earlier slip. "Right. I'll go think about dinner. You get on with your next masterpiece."

She was still staring after him as he hurried away. He could feel her gaze drilling into the back of his head, but he ignored it, trying to shake the lingering tendrils of that strange sharp anger in him away once more. He cut up the carrots and potatoes, perhaps slightly harder than necessary as he prepped the dinner, but by the time everything was in the oven, he was almost back to himself again.

He poked his head around Sophie's door. "Dinner's in five minutes. Hey! What's this? Sophie, are you finally *reading* a *book?* I thought you'd forgotten how to!"

She stuck her tongue out, clasping the book to her chest in just the same way that Abs always did. John's spine went cold as he recognised the cover.

He fumbled a hand for his pocket and found it empty.

"Sophie! Give that to me now! It's not a toy! You can't just help yourself to other people's things!"

Sophie startled, shocked at his sudden anger. The look of fear on her face startled him out of his sudden rage. He never shouted at the kids. His dad had always veered towards authoritarianism growing up, and John had sworn he wouldn't end up the same way. He didn't even know why he was so angry, really, just that there was a strange jealousy overtaking him for the contents of the nook, one he could neither explain nor control.

He perched on the end of the bed and took the book from her hands. She held it tightly for a second, as if she was going to tug it back again but then released it.

"Sorry, love," he murmured. "I shouldn't have shouted. But this book is very, very old and we need to take care of it. We can't just treat it like any other book on the shelf, alright?"

"Well, why did you leave it on my bed then?" she said sullenly. "If you didn't want me to read it, you shouldn't have left it for me."

John looked at her sharply. Sophie could be many things—moody, quick to anger, occasionally self-absorbed in that way teenagers often were—but she wasn't a liar.

"It must have fallen out of my pocket by mistake. Your mother probably got confused and thought it was yours, that's all. Although I don't know why she would. Max is the reader, not you."

Sophie stuck her tongue out again, and John grinned. She seemed to have forgiven him for his outburst, at least.

"Besides, there's no point you hanging on to it," he pointed out. "It's not like you can read it anyway."

"*Dad,* enough. I know how to read, alright? It's not my fault phones hadn't been invented in your day!"

"Hey! I'm not that old! And anyway, I didn't mean it like that, I just meant it's all written in an old-fashioned way, before they invented proper spelling and when they had weird curvy handwriting." He smirked at her. "You'd need a scholar or an academic to translate it, probably."

She gave him an odd look and snatched the book back.

"Sophie! I just told you—"

But she had already flicked it open and began to read.

"Goody Abevan's fore tooth was full sore with a tooth worm," she read. "I had given to her a measure of hensbane to smoke for the pain, but she had said that it was not enough to stymie the ailment. I made her a charm to wear beneath her small clothes and a poultice of daisy roots mashed in vinegar. I bade her come back upon next week if the ailment persisted."

She closed the book with a triumphant snap, her smug expression not that much different than Max's had been.

John gaped at her wordlessly.

She shrugged one shoulder. "It's an old herb-wife's journal. It's really interesting, Dad, all about the different cures she used and the village ailments. I've only just started, but it's amazing stuff. It's like I'm there with her." Her face was bright and beaming, all traces of the habitual sullen pout it had worn of late washed away. "The bit I've just got to is about a spate of bad luck they were having in the village. She's written down all the charms she's tried to lift it so far, but nothing has worked. People are starting to whisper, she says, and the new miller, Llewelyn, wants to send off for a witchfinder general. If things don't improve soon, she thinks he'll get his way, and that frightens her."

Cerys did say there was an aura of fear in that room.

If the witchfinder general had been sent for, I suppose they would have been afraid...

John shook his head, forcefully. He was getting just as bad as Abs.

"Well, your eyes are clearly better than mine then," he grumbled, still eyeing the book uneasily. He hadn't been able to decipher a word of it. He hadn't even been sure it had been written in English, honestly. "Alright, if it thrills you that much, you can keep it, just for today. But, Sophie, you *must* take care of it. This is irreplaceable. It's a piece of history!"

"I know, Dad. I'll be careful," she said, hugging it to her chest gleefully.

John wandered back to the kitchen to set the table, his thoughts still churning. He'd have to take another look at the book. Perhaps Sophie was just better at translating it than he was. After all, Shakespeare was written in early modern English, and they learnt that at school, didn't they? Maybe she was just better trained at the kind of mental agility needed to translate on the go.

But we're not in England, he thought suddenly. *Would they have even written in English here? Wouldn't it be written in Welsh? And how likely was it that a local herb-wife could even write in that era?*

A sudden realisation crested over him with a surge of disappointment. It was all a hoax. Of *course*, it was! There were too many anomalies for it to be anything else. Someone, or perhaps some people, unknown, had for some reason best known to themselves set up this elaborate joke.

Maybe even Cerys? She did say that her kids couldn't afford to live here anymore...

But they had seven years to buy the mill if they wanted it. And it wasn't at a bad Waterhouse...?

He shook his head again, trying to dislodge the disappointment growing there. Some small part of him had *wanted* it all to be true, that was the trouble.

"Still," he murmured aloud, getting the dinner out of the oven. "It makes a good story."

John huffed and puffed, trying in vain to get comfortable in bed that night. The incessant scratch, screech and splash of that blessed waterwheel was an exquisite kind of torture. He held the pillow firmly over his head, but the noise seemed, impossibly, to get louder—as if it was trapped inside his head. Abbie, beside him, didn't seem bothered by it in the slightest. She twitched slightly, frowning through her dreams, but she didn't wake.

He scrunched his eyes tight shut, trying to block it out, but it was impossible.

I'm going to rip that thing down with my bare hands in a minute. No wonder the previous owners kept having accidents. They were probably all loopy from sleep deprivation. First thing tomorrow, I'm buying myself some earplugs.

He blew out a breath, pummelled the pillow again and then stared up at the ceiling, abandoning sleep as a lost cause. A crack of moonlight slipped through the curtains, slashing sharply across the ceiling above him. The trees outside swayed in the wind, their limbs cutting through the moonlight in jagged lines of black. They looked almost like people, dancing in time to the breeze. There, that branch could be an arm, raised as if to strike, and that one, with the cluster of twigs on the end, looked like it was holding up a burning torch.

The creaking grew louder. It was a strange thing, but combined with those spectral, disembodied limbs flashing through the moonlight, it almost seemed like footsteps creaking the floorboards. As if the people baying outside, eager to be let in, thirsty for violence, were getting closer.

A light flashed. A creak at the door. Two large, dark eyes were illuminated far too close, staring straight at him. He sat up with a yelp, panting and cursing through the black.

"Dad!" Sophie hissed beside him, and he saw it was only her after all, lingering in the threshold of his bedroom, lit only by her phone torch light. Her eyes were wide and frightened, a thin sheen of sweat prickling her skin. He started to breathe again, laughing a little at his own over-active imagination.

"What is it?"

"There's someone in my room."

John was out of bed in seconds, all laughter dropping from his lips immediately. He didn't have much he could use as a weapon in here, so he snatched up the roller-blind he still hadn't attached to the bathroom windows as he stormed past. The lights in Sophie's room were on, but the room was empty. The cupboard too, and there was no one under the bed. He tried the window, it was locked.

"Stay here," he snapped. "I'll go check the doors downstairs."

But they were all locked too. The house was still and quiet, save for the incessant creak of that damned wheel. He dropped the roller blind with a clunk that echoed through the sleeping rooms and trudged back up to Sophie. She was curled up on her bed, her back pressed against the wall, terror in her eyes.

He perched next to her. "No one there," he said. "A nightmare, do you think? Too much reading about witchcraft, poultices and potions, maybe?"

"I *felt* him."

"Him?" John said sharply.

Sophie nodded, tearfully. "He was there, by the end of my bed, standing, staring down at me. I couldn't say anything. I couldn't move. I wanted him to disappear, but I just froze. Then, slowly, he pulled the cover away and he touched my leg. His hands were so cold, Dad, sweaty and icy and hard. I screamed and kicked away at him, and he just fled."

John reached for her, pulling her into a tight hug, pressing a kiss against her head. "I didn't hear you scream, Soph," he murmured. "None of it really happened. It was a nightmare, nothing more."

"My blankets were all on the floor!" she said angrily.

"Yeah, because they fell off in the night, and you felt the cold and dreamed that someone stole them."

"I'm not lying!"

"Don't shout at me, Sophie, you'll wake the others. I'm not saying it wasn't utterly terrifying, because it certainly sounds it, but it was just a nightmare, that's all."

She looked at him, half angry, half hopeful, as if simultaneously furious that she wasn't believed and desperate to be persuaded that it was nothing but a fantasy after all. He squeezed her even more tightly, as if he could squeeze all the bad dreams right out of her.

"I don't want to go back to sleep," she murmured into his chest at last. "I don't want another bad dream."

He checked his watch. It was five a.m. He rubbed his eyes.

"Fine," he murmured. "Why don't you watch something light-hearted and silly on your laptop to distract yourself. The wi-fi should be working by now. But put your headphones in, so you don't wake Max, alright?"

She nodded and slipped away, and he trudged back to bed himself. He would never get back to sleep again either now, he knew, but he couldn't bear to get up for the day either yet. He settled back into bed beside Abbie, glancing over at her.

It wasn't like her not to wake up when the kids had nightmares. For one paranoid moment, he wondered if she might have died in her sleep, and he slipped a tentative hand over for her to check. No, still breathing, though her skin was freezing cold and sweat slicked.

Can it be menopause, already? Doesn't that give you night sweats? But Abs isn't that old. I would have thought she had a few more years before that set in. Unless it's some sort of early-onset menopause? Maybe that would explain the mood swings and the paranoia, too?

He gently pushed her hair out of her face. Her eyes shot open. She gasped. Clutching at her throat, she fumbled a wild hand out for John. He snagged it instantly, pulling her into his arms.

"It's just a nightmare. Just a nightmare," he murmured again and again, rocking her stiff and shivering body until she had calmed at last. "Was it that cat, again? Do you want to talk about it?"

But she just shook her head fiercely.

"Sophie didn't sleep well last night either. It must be something in the air here," he offered. "She's plugged in to her laptop now."

"No, she's not," Abbie said hoarsely, stumbling out of bed and running barefoot out of the door.

"What do you mean, Abs? Of course she is. She—"

But Abbie had already gone. John jogged after

her, down the stairs, out of the door, back to the millpond Abbie was so obsessed with—

—and found Sophie there by the waters' edge, staring in the swirling ripples.

How had Abs known she was here? She'd only just woken up! She couldn't have heard her leaving, could she?

"Sophie! What are you doing out here with no coat or shoes on at this time in the morning? I thought you were watching a TV programme," he snapped at her. He hadn't even heard her leave her room, even if Abbie had somehow managed to.

And surely I ought to have heard the front door opening?

Sophie barely seemed to hear him. She was staring into the centre of the pond. The black waters were reflected in her wide gaze.

It's always that millpond. They're both obsessed with it.

"I am going to drain that whole blessed pool dry," he roared. "I am going to pump it down to the silty depths and then fill the whole damned thing in with concrete!"

His words swam, distorted, over the undulating surface. *Down to the depths. Damned, damned, down to the depths.*

Neither Sophie nor Abbie flinched. Sophie had had a growth spurt over the past few months and now they stood, of a height, the two women together, side by side, staring into the waters. They had the same short chestnut hair and the same dark eyes, and it seemed to John then that they were almost an uncanny mirror of each other. The early dawn breeze tugged at them all, sending a chill right through John, rustling Abbie and Sophie's clothes as if it wanted to pull them into the middle of the pond too. John wanted to pull them away, but somehow, he couldn't. His feet were frozen to the ground. Anger swelled up in him irresistibly once more.

It's her fault. She started this. Everything would be better again if she just stopped. If I could just make her stop.

The thought frightened him with its vehemence. He curled his hands into fists, digging his nails deep into his palms to ground himself.

There's no point playing the blame game. We're a team, he told himself fiercely. *We're in this together.*

He was struggling to believe it though. Abbie seemed so utterly apart from him now, holding tightly onto Sophie's hand, staring into the surface of the millpond.

"There's a woman in the water," Abbie murmured.

"Yes," Sophie agreed softly.

"Abbie, Sophie, stop that now," he ordered, but they didn't even seem to hear him.

"She doesn't want to be there."

"No."

"I said stop it! Come back inside. It's far too early for these games!" He was shouting now, his voice swelling up in impotent rage, spiralling far more quickly than he meant it to. He tried to tug them away, but neither of them moved.

"There is anger here, and fear. Hatred," Abbie's voice was so low it was barely more than a whisper.

John shivered. He tried to think of some calm, reasonable, logical argument that would make all this better again, but the only thing left in his mind was a fizzing, crackling static anger—a thunderstorm of rage drowning out all conscious thought.

But even that animal wrath disappeared as Sophie turned to him at last. Her eyes were almost as black as the dim pre-dawn gloom around them. "And revenge," she whispered.

CHAPTER 5
THE CURSE OF THE MILL

Abbie's head was pounding. John hadn't spoken to her all morning. She didn't know why. There was anger in him now. She could feel it, simmering there beneath the surface constantly. He had never been an angry man before.

That's what this place does. It brings out the anger and cruelty of men, and the pain and fear of women.

John hadn't let them discuss the woman in the water. He didn't want to *encourage* them, he said—or feed their fears.

But Abbie wasn't afraid anymore. She had been terrified, truly, bone-deep blind with panic when she had first come—when she had first seen the shadow, when the cat had seeped out of her dreams into her house, when she had first felt the malevolence emanating from the chilly air around the pool.

But now, she was *furious.*

She would have stormed into the pond right then and there if she thought it would have done any good, but the breeze had shifted and the woman in the water had transformed back into the shadow of algae and pondweed. The hold on Abbie was gone and the moment was too. So, she had brought Sophie back inside instead and made her a large mug of hot chocolate to warm up, sending her off for a shower and breakfast before Max woke up.

She'd taken a pill for the headache, but it hadn't shifted. She hadn't had food. Couldn't sit down to eat. Didn't want anything. Had no hunger left in her, just a strange restlessness fizzing inside her. She tried to do some laundry, but found herself staring blankly into the washing basket, unsure what to do with the clothes. She tried to get started on some dinner prep for tonight, but caught herself standing in the middle of the kitchen with a vegetable knife, staring into space. Time kept skipping, it seemed, distraction tugging at the corners of her mind whenever she stopped moving for a moment.

As if it is out there, waiting to catch up with me as soon as I drop my guard...

John barged through the kitchen, slamming doors and cupboards as he got himself a cuppa. He didn't ask her if she wanted one, as he usually did. Didn't even ask her what she was doing. Didn't say anything to her, in fact. He eyed the knife in her hand, and for one awful moment she thought he was considering snatching it off her or holding it to her throat.

Don't be ridiculous, Abbie, she told herself firmly. *That's not the sort of man John is. He doesn't have a single violent bone in his body.*

But she put the knife back in the kitchen drawer hastily and shut it away from temptation all the same. As John turned to get the milk out of the fridge, she drifted to the studio instead, away from the weighty silence of his wrath. The sketch of the shadow lady stared back at her from the art table in the centre of the studio. She had been thinking of making the sculpture in black iron and chains—perhaps even embedding it in the millpond itself as a memorial, but it was all wrong now, she could see that. The shadow woman had already been a victim of some sort, Abbie was sure about that, even if she didn't know the details of how or why. The woman in the water didn't need to be memorialised in her fear forever. She deserved more than that.

The door to the studio slammed open and John stormed across the floor to the little nook at the far end of the room, still ignoring her. She thinned her lips. It wasn't like him to give her the silent treatment. He was normally a fierce advocate for talking about their problems before they grew too big.

"What are you doing?" she asked.

"I'm taking the artefacts we found to the local Heritage Museum," he snapped, coming back out with handfuls of fabric wrapped bundles which he stuffed into an old carrier bag. "I thought if anybody would know what they were or what to do with them, they would."

His tone prickled at her. She could feel herself bristling under the weight of it.

"Why are you so cross with me?" she demanded.

He threw up his hands with a feral growl. "Because, Abs, you started this whole thing, and now it's impacted Sophie too! She was perfectly fine before you started getting in her head!"

Abbie narrowed her eyes at him, the injustice of this scalding over her skin. "We were all alright before you insisted on dragging us out here in the first place, you mean!"

He roared again, and she flinched a little. "Dragging! This was our dream, Abs, sorry for trying to make it a reality!"

"It's *your* dream," she snapped back, slamming a hand on the paint-stained table. The old jam jar she used as a watercolour pot twitched as the table rattled, threatening to fall and spill its murky paint-water everywhere. "It's always been *your* dream. You are the one who is so obsessed with owning your own gallery! Everything, all the time, is working towards that. You're always pushing me to sell my art, everything I ever make, so we can squirrel away the money for your grand designs! You moved us all out here because you couldn't afford to accomplish your dreams in London. You're always talking about how successful the gallery will be, and how much money it is going to make. Well, maybe some of us don't do art for the money we can make from it."

He blushed fiercely at that, but his lip curled back in a sneer. "Oh, no, I forgot you were far too high-minded and artist to care about anything as prosaic as eating and drinking, paying the rent, feeding your children, and making their house warm and safe." He ticked them all off on his fingers as he ranted, then jabbed an accusatory finger in her direction. "You hid in the studio all day yesterday indulging your creative and left me to do all the mundane activities that actually keep this household working alone!"

She leapt to her feet, her temper soaring. "Hey! That's not fair! You told me to work! You said you were happy to do the dinner, and I should just get on with it!"

He bellowed at her wordlessly, snatched up the water filled jam jar and threw it hard against the wall. She flinched as it splintered into a dozen different shards. The water dripped slowly down the wall, tangled in the rusty wheel which dominated the room.

They both panted for second. Numb disbelief made every inch of her body icy. John had never been violent. Never raised his voice. To start smashing and breaking things now...

And how long before he escalates? It's just water pots now, but where does it end?

He moved towards her, but she moved away, not meeting his eyes.

"Abs," he said hoarsely. "Abs, I'm so sorry, I don't know what came over me, I—"

"Just get out," she snapped, pushing him away as he tried to slip his arms around her waist. "Go to your precious museum! And don't come back until you're sane again!"

He let out a bitter, hollow laugh. "Can't you see the irony in that, Abbie?"

But he walked away all the same.

She collapsed to the floor, weeping, as soon as she heard the front door slam and the roar of the car engine carrying him away. It took her a little while to pull herself back together again. When the tears finally abated, she found herself shivering and exhausted, as if she had been hollowed out. Numbly, she shuffled over to the fragments of the shattered glass water pot, and carefully gathered them, but her fingers felt so unwieldy now that she nicked herself on their jagged edges. Fresh red blood welled up, slipping across her fingers. She stared at it. It reflected strangely off the glass shards of the jam jar, distorting in the curved fragments.

Does it always have to end in blood?

She wasn't quite sure where that thought came from. It sat, stone-like, in the back of her mind and she couldn't shift it, even as she tipped the glass carefully into the bin. Slowly, she stared at the dark shadow at the back of the room, the smashed entrance to that hidden nook.

Perhaps I should have seen the violence lingering suppressed in him earlier. Did he not rip down that wall with his bare hands? Perhaps the anger was always hidden within him, just waiting to be brought to the surface.

As if in a trance, she shuffled towards that gloomy recess.

What other secrets are you hiding? she asked it silently. *And, more importantly, what other secrets will you reveal?*

She took another hesitant step forwards and peered inside. It was hollow within, empty, as if all traces of its earlier character had been washed away. The tools were gone, the cat, gone, the book, gone.

But a flicker of sunlight from the room behind her glinted off something lurking in the shadows. She edged her way in and crouched down to examine it.

The mirror remained, lurking in the corner, winking at her in the dim light.

John must have overlooked it.

But even as she thought it, she knew it was a lie. This mirror *wanted* her to find it. It needed her to find it. It was calling to her now.

Carefully, she picked it up. It was smashed in the middle as if something heavy had landed right in the centre of it, and it looked almost cobweb-like to her mind.

Everything is still woven together. It is still connected.

That meant something, she knew, if only she could decipher what.

Distantly, she ran her thumb over the fractured surface, as if she could melt it back into one piece once more with just a little tenderness. Her blood smeared across the fragments.

Abbie almost dropped the mirror then. Beneath the faint pink smudge of blood, a shadow moved.

∼

Anglesey wasn't that big. According to Max's blessed guidebook, you could drive around the whole thing in two hours. But the journey to the heritage museum seemed interminable to John that morning.

He had *never* lost his temper like that. Had never deliberately broken something or tried to scare his wife on purpose.

Abbie and Sophie aren't the only ones losing control at the moment. Only Max is immune, it seems. Probably because he's so oblivious to the stress of the move, buried in his book.

Guilt swirled through his stomach again. The farther that he drove away, the more shame overwhelmed him. His anger had seemed so natural, so just and inevitable, at the time, but now he was beginning to question his own sanity.

But she did provoke me. She said some awful things. It wasn't entirely my fault, was it?

Something insidious crawled beneath his skin, making him feel oddly nauseous, as if the air was greasy now, and he was sucking down slippery lungfuls of it.

Don't start down that road, he told himself firmly. *Don't blame her for losing your temper.*

He tapped his fingers against the steering wheel, jittering uneasily.

But the gallery wasn't just my dream, was it? I thought we both wanted it. I haven't selfishly uprooted our whole lives just for my own needs. She just said that because she was angry, didn't she? She didn't really mean it...

The guilt wormed its way deeper into his stomach, bringing out another, reactive wave of anger with it.

"Well, she should have said something earlier, if she didn't want to come," he snapped out loud and then sighed again. Getting angry was no good, he knew it, but they seemed so entrenched in this insanity now that it was difficult to see a way out of it.

He pulled into the somewhat neglected carpark of the little heritage museum at last, snatched the carrier bag out of the passenger seat, and tried to rearrange his face into a smile as he pushed his way inside.

"Hello," he said to the old lady behind the visitor information desk. "My name is John Harper, and I've got a bit of a strange query for you today, I'm afraid. I've found some old artefacts in my new house as we were doing renovations. I wondered if you could tell me a bit about them, please."

"Oh, I don't know about that stuff," the lady said anxiously twiddling with her rather lurid name badge. "I just do the tickets and the gift shop till, really. Hang on a moment now. You'd best wait here. I'll get Nicole. She'll be the best person to ask about that kind of thing."

She doddered off through a back door and John lingered in the gift shop-come-ticket office, staring around. There were tea-towels of the Menai Suspension Bridge and the Britannia Bridge, a selection of

DVDs featuring Dawn French, who was apparently born near here, some plush puffins with *Puffin Island* embroidered on their chest, and various magnets loudly declaring *Anglesey the best place to be*!

In the far corner was a shelf of witchy paraphernalia, ranging from history books about the Anglesey witch trials, to rubbers shaped like cauldrons, to garish solar-powered plastic witches that nodded merrily at you if you left them in the sun. He couldn't help but wonder what the poor women who had been dunked, burned, crushed or hanged at the mere accusation of witchcraft would make of such tacky mementos, but he kept his thoughts to himself. The heritage centre probably didn't bring in a lot of money. They'd probably sell anything they could to keep the lights on.

He turned as the back door opened again. A younger woman in a neat arran sweater, her blonde hair gathered up in a claw clip, came hurrying out with a grin. She had a firm handshake and a nice smile.

"Mr Harper? I'm Dr Nicole Waterhouse. Sue said you had some artefacts for us to look at? Why don't you come through to the back and we'll take a peek at them."

He followed her through the back door to a

chilly room beyond. Tall, locked cupboards dominated three of the walls and stacks of cardboard boxes held the fourth hostage, towering precariously around the sink and kitchen counter that Nicole headed to. A large table sat directly beneath a fizzing strip of fluorescent lighting.

"Tea?" Nicole asked as John carefully unpacked the bag. She brought back two mugs of strong tea and picked eagerly at the treasures John unwrapped. "Well now, let's see what we've got. Where did you say you found them again?"

"We were renovating our house and found it behind a stud wall. I just wondered if you could tell me a bit more about them, really."

"Well, the poor kitty isn't really my area of expertise, I'm afraid. I did my doctorate in folklore and health in the early modern period and mummifying cats falls a little out of that area. But these now, these I can tell you all about." She beamed as she carefully pulled the tools towards her. "You see this knife is carved with runes? That suggests it is an herb-wife's blade and would put its origin between 1650 and 1675, I believe. There was a tradition around that time that bad herbs could infect a blade and sully any charms or poultices, so they carved these symbols into the blade to ward away bad spirits and keep their potions clear. And this pestle still has some staining around the curve, if you look carefully." She tilted it towards him so that he could get a better look. "A dark stain like that would possibly be from repeated exposure to yew berries. They are highly poisonous, of course, and wouldn't be used in traditional medicines."

"So, the owner tried to kill people then?" he guessed.

Nicole laughed at that. "Well, possibly, but I doubt it. They were more often used in death rites. Some people believed that they could be used to capture spirits—or draw them back if one wanted to."

"What, like ghosts?" he asked uneasily.

She laughed again. "Something similar. There is a certain logic to it, I suppose. After all, they were aware that yew berries caused death when ingested, so they connected them to death in all forms, I suppose. It was considered good luck, for instance, for a funeral procession to pass by a yew tree—which is why you see so many of them in graveyards, and wands of yew were often used by druids to banish evil spirits. People believed a lot more fervently in that sort of thing at the time."

John eyed the dark stain uneasily. "And this

one?" he asked, gesturing towards what he had assumed was a tiny milling stone.

Nicole's face lit up. "These are some of my favourite bits of folklore," she confided. "Look, I have one myself." She fished out a necklace from under her jumper, a smooth round stone with a hole in the centre, through which she had threaded a thin chain. "They have lots of names, Adder stones, witch stones, fairy stones. They're commonly called *Glain Neidr* or *Maen Magi* in Welsh, and appear in the Mabinogion twice—though no one can agree quite what they're supposed to do. In one old Arthurian legend, they turned Sir Gawain invisible, but mine has never done that for me. They're just generically magical, I suppose."

"So, this is all a witch's stuff, then?" he asked carefully. Cerys had been right about that at least then, it seemed. "I thought it might be to do with milling and things, seeing as we found it in a mill."

"Well, herb-craft and superstitions were very much a part of everyday life back then," she explained. "There's nothing to say that the miller's wife or daughter couldn't have taken an interest in such things. Do you mind if we keep these things? They'll be invaluable for our collection."

"Fine," he murmured, his mind racing. He

chewed his lip, hesitated and then reluctantly pulled out the book too. It was probably a hoax anyway, but it might be as well to hear the confirmation out loud. Then he could put the whole thing to bed and rest easy.

He slid the book across the table towards her. She leant forwards, her hair falling into her face as she peered at it.

"What's this now? This is a remarkably intact version of a book, if the timing is the same as the tools. Hang on, I'll need some gloves for this one, I think." She hurried to a drawer and pulled out some thin white kid gloves and carefully negotiated the book open. Her eyes went wide as she opened the front cover and read the title page.

"I don't believe it," she murmured, glancing at him with wide, wondering eyes. "Where did you say you found it again?"

"In a hidden room in an old mill."

"A mill!" Her whole face lit up with eager anticipation. She was practically vibrating with excitement now. "Hang on a moment, don't touch anything!" She dashed through another door, calling for her colleagues. A balding middle-aged man also scurried in, pulling on some gloves and even Sue from the gift shop came bustling in from the other direction, eager to see what the commotion was about.

"This is Richard Morgen, he's the managing director of the heritage museum and the resident expert on Catrin Waterhouse. Richard, I think you're going to want to see this," Nicole said giddily.

They huddled around the table, half edging a very perplexed John out.

"The paper looks from the right time period, and the ink. And the language used too doesn't seem anachronistic," Nicole said in a hushed voice. "It could be genuine. We could arrange a scan for it to be sure."

"Surely Catrin Waterhouse would not have written it herself, though? That would change a great deal of what we know about her," Richard murmured with a small frown.

"No, here, on the title page. *Written as told to her by the fair hand of Beth Miller.*" Nicole stared excitedly at her colleagues. "It was dictated to Beth Miller, as in Llewelyn Miller's niece, do you think? The one she was accused of bewitching?"

A frisson of excitement ran around the room, but John was just left feeling confounded. "Sorry, what's going on?"

Nicole beamed at him. "You've just brought us

the most exciting discovery of the year, if it turns out to be genuine. The woman who dictated this journal, Catrin Waterhouse, was the last known victim of the Witchfinder General, Matthew , in Anglesey. There was a spate of various misfortunes which the locals put down to witchcraft and curses, so they sent for him. He accused Catrin Waterhouse, a midwife, herb-wife and, by then, quite an old woman, of seducing several young women—including Beth Miller—into wickedness and witchcraft, but no proof could be found. Catrin was ducked in the millpond and was found guilty. She confessed then, I suppose because she knew that they were going to kill her anyway, but she took all the blame, saying Beth was innocent. She was drowned in the same millpond they had dunked her in, and everyone thought it would be the end of it. But that very same night, the miller—who had been the one to persuade the village to send for in the first place—and the witchfinder General himself, both died in mysterious circumstances. Everyone said it was Catrin's revenge. If this book of herbal remedies *was* written by Beth Miller, it's proof that they did have some sort of relationship!"

John stared at them. "But you're not saying that they really were witches, are you? You're not saying this Catrin Waterhouse really had anything to do with their deaths?"

But his gaze drifted back to the pestle all the same, still stained with crushed yew berries from all those years ago...

Nicole laughed. "I'm not saying she hexed Llewellyn Miller or Matthew to death, no. The way that we understand certain things and the way that they would have can be quite different. But she probably did believe in some sort of things which we might classify in this era as 'magic'. I suspect it would have been a white magic, rather than black and deadly arts though. And I think it quite possible that the stress of the dunking, and perhaps his own guilty conscience, instigated a stroke or an aneurism or a heart-attack or similar in Llewellyn Miller. Although I doubt the same could be said of Matthew . I don't think witchfinder generals had consciences to prick," she added wryly.

John went to pick up the book again, but she secured her hand across his wrist fiercely. "I'm sorry, this belongs to the museum now. We cannot let you have it back until we have authenticated it and discovered whether it is genuine or not. We'll need to send it off for various tests of its authenticity which we can't perform here, scans and ink samples and the like. It'll be a while before any of us see it again. If it is the real thing, it will need to be kept here in special conditions to alleviate any possible deterioration."

He blushed. Of course they would keep it, if it was genuine. He should have expected that. He didn't really know why he had reached for it, only that he hadn't been able to help himself. But he nodded tightly.

Perhaps that is for the best. We'll wash our hands of all of it.

"We'll put it up on display once we've properly examined, secured and digitised it," Richard said kindly. "And we'll put your name down as the donor. You can come back in and see it on display any time you like. We'll organise a free season ticket for you and your family. You can do that can't you, Sue?" he prompted, and Sue nodded eagerly, but John wasn't listening.

He glanced down at the book once more. "You said that the language was era-appropriate," he said slowly. "It must have taken you a long time to learn. People couldn't just pick it up and read it, could they?"

Nicole laughed. "Most Welsh speakers can understand late modern Welsh with a bit of work, it's the handwriting that makes you think. As a relatively wealthy and influential figure, it is not entirely surprising that Beth learned some reading and writing—around ten percent of women were literate in this era, compared to around thirty percent of men. But, she chose to write in Welsh, even though after the 1536 Act of Union law and 1650 commission into Education by Oliver Cromwell, she would also have been taught English. I suggest that this was a deliberate attempt to hide the contents of the book from the Witchfinder General, who, of course, came over from England." She spoke as if she was presenting her next thesis already, and John could only blink at her.

"Or, if Catrin was dictating in Welsh, perhaps she found it easier just to write it as she heard it, rather than translate it as she was writing it," Richard suggested, his eyes gleaming. "I could easily see a conference paper in this. Maybe a journal article too. The *London Folklore* journal is fairly prestigious, and I know the editor. Or *Mythlore* has a good reputation too."

"Either way—" Nicole began, but Sue cut across her, nodding towards John.

"Look at that poor man's face. He doesn't need an academic lecture," she chided, clucking her tongue. "Sorry, they're impossible to stop when they get going," she added apologetically to John. "I don't understand half the things they say, sometimes."

But John wasn't listening.

It was written in *Welsh*. In Welsh. In late modern Welsh, according to Nicole—which Sophie would have no way of translating. No way at all of knowing.

Maybe she just made it up to mess with me?

But Sophie had mentioned the spate of bad luck and the imminent arrival of the witchfinder general. She could have had no way of knowing about that either, unless she had read it.

Maybe she's secretly been learning Welsh with Max, so she can assimilate more easily here?

But that thought sounded hopeless and ridiculous even in his own head. Even if it were true—an unlikely possibility—she'd never had learned enough in the short time since she'd been told they were moving here to translate an old witch's book.

He stumbled to his feet. "Thank you for your help," he murmured. "I'll be back soon."

"If you want to know more about Catrin Waterhouse, you could check out the local library or the local county records," Nicole said, showing him to the door, still beaming. "She's a bit of a local legend around here. I'm sure you'll find plenty of information on her."

"And there's a pamphlet on her in the gift shop," Sue called after him cheerily. "Only a quid. A real bargain!"

And with this endorsement still ringing in his ears, John stumbled dazedly back to the car.

JOHN DIDN'T REALISE he'd been driving in circles until he passed the chip shop on the corner for the third time. He shook his head, trying to clear it, and forced himself to concentrate until he had taken the correct turning down the slope towards their little house.

It was impossible. It was all utterly, ridiculously impossible.

But Nicole and Richard were clearly well-educated people. And they seemed genuinely thrilled by the discovery. They would recognise a hoax, wouldn't they?

The gate was left open, swinging on its hinge in the breeze, so John just guided the car straight down the slope and parked up, right beside the millpond. He didn't get out, though. He couldn't. What on earth would he say to Abs? That she was right? That there was something unnatural going on here?

He sat there, drumming his numb fingers

against the steering wheel until the windscreen had misted with condensation from his breath and the skies beyond bled with sunset hues. The whole car still smelt of stale water and damp from its untimely dip in the millpond. He should probably get it professionally valeted really, but he didn't know where he could do that around here.

He was staring at the misty windscreen before him, but it was Nicole's expression that he saw once more. She had truly believed it was this Catrin Waterhouse's book, and this Miller girl's handwriting. She wouldn't have been so excited if she thought that it was a hoax.

Slowly, John opened the car door. He walked right up to the edge of the pond, the crunch of dead leaves and gravel underfoot echoed through the still air. He stared into the surface of the murky water. The afternoon light glinted back at him from the dancing, swirling currents.

The pond should have been painted the bloody shades of the dying light above it, surely, awash with reflections of umbers, golds and faint pinky blushes. But it was as midnight and impenetrable as ever.

He peered right into the centre of it, where Abbie and Sophie had been so transfixed this morning. He saw nothing. Not even the faintest outline of a shadow, a hint of a suggestion, nothing that could even be mistaken for a woman in a poor light.

Maybe we should just drain it?

He had said it this morning in anger, but the thought occurred to him now once again.

Get rid of it all. Purge it. Make it clean and pure once more.

He blinked. Pure? Ha. He doubted the mouldering little mill would be 'pure' now if you blowtorched it.

Perhaps its better to leave the pond anyway. If there is something sinister here, it might be best to have it all trapped in one place...

Another wave of anger swept through him, inexplicably.

"Alright," he said loudly, feeling somewhat foolish. "If you *are* real, show yourself. Prove it."

Of course, nothing happened. His own voice was the only thing to bounce back at him from the murky surface of the waters.

He nodded tightly. "Fine," he spat out through clenched teeth. "Good. Then we're done with this nonsense once and for all."

He barged his way indoors, slamming the front door open so hard it dented the wall behind it. Some small part of him at the back of his mind was protesting that he was not behaving either rationally or calmly, but he didn't care anymore. He burst into the studio, making Abbie yelp.

"Get Sophie in here now," he barked. "Max too. Get everyone."

Abbie looked for a second as if she wanted to argue, but he glared at her, and she seemed to think better of it. She scuttled from the room with her head down, and a wave of shame seared across his chest—but it only made his anger rise higher in response, as if she was deliberately provoking him. She had started this whole thing, and now she was making him out to be the monster here.

He grabbed his hammer and swung it at the remains of the stud wall. It crumbled beneath the weight of his righteous anger, spitting splinters to the floor. But it wasn't falling fast enough for his liking. He flung the hammer aside, and it clattered and spun across the floor. With a roar, he ripped down the remaining chunks of wall with his bare hands until nothing at all remained except rubble and the dancing dust motes hovering like smog in the air around him.

He whirled around. His shadow stretched out

long before him, staining the floorboards black in the panting silence.

Abbie stood in the doorway, one arm protectively clasping Sophie, the other around Max. All three of them were staring at him in pallid, mute fear, as if *he* were the mad one!

"We are done with it all now," he growled at them ferally. "I don't want to hear *anyone* in this house mentioning witchcraft, or herb-books, strange shadows or voices, unsettling nightmares or any damned ghosts ever again. Do you understand? It's *done.*"

He glared at them all.

Abbie's hands were whiter even that her face as she clutched the children closer, but she let out a small, terse nod. The children did too.

"Good. I am going to bed and when I wake up in the morning, we are going to start afresh. No nightmares. No mysteries. Happy families all round. Yes?"

Again, mutely, they nodded.

He kicked the rubble at his feet hard, sending it skittering across the floor like frightened mice, and Abbie flinched.

"This is our home now," he growled to whichever malevolent spirits might happen to be listening. "And if you want to chase us out of it, you're going to have to do a damned sight better than that."

The slam of the door as he stormed away again echoed through the whole house. And John couldn't help but think like it sounded a little like a bellowing, mocking laugh...

CHAPTER 6
THE MIRROR'S REFLECTION

There was a spectral feline hiss echoing closer to her ear as the slam of the car door outside echoed abruptly through the house. Abbie flinched. Silently thankful for the warning, she hastily squirrelled her treasure back into its wrappings, shoved it into the bottom of the box, threw some fabric scraps over the top to hide it and all but flung it under the bed, pulling the empty suitcase in front of it hastily. She got to her feet, brushed down her smock and was halfway down the stairs again before John had even opened the front door.

"Morning!" she said, a little too brightly. "The kids went into school alright then, did they?"

John gave her a grin she almost believed. "Well,

they're both safely ensconced in their classes now, but I can't say they're happy about it. If Sophie slouched through the school gates any slower, she'd have been going backwards." His smile wavered a little. "Honestly, love, I would have thought they would have settled in by now. Do you think we ought to phone up the school and ask for a teacher, parent conference to see if they're alright?"

"It's only been three weeks," she said. "It takes time to make new friends and settle into a new routine. If they're still struggling after Christmas, we'll phone. Besides, you know we'll only hopelessly embarrass Sophie if we're seen within a five-mile radius of her friends. We'd have to sneak into the school incognito."

John snorted out a laugh at that. "At least she's made some new friends now."

"She was always going to. She's a sweet girl. She'll be fine."

"Max hasn't mentioned any other friends yet," he said, giving her an anxious glance.

She smiled. "No. Well, Max has always had a little more trouble adjusting to new people, hasn't he? But he doesn't seem too unhappy."

He squinted at her suspiciously. "What's going on here, Abs?"

A flare of panic shot across her chest immediately, and her mind flew back up to the little box beneath the bed. She squawked out a trill of unconvincing laughter. "What do you mean?"

He slung an arm over her shoulder and pulled her into half a hug. "Well, you're usually the one worrying about everything, and I'm normally the one consoling you. When did we switch places?"

She laughed again, more genuinely this time, relief bringing joy organically to her lips, and allowed him to press a kiss to her temple.

Of course, the answer was right in front of him, if he had only wanted to see it. Ever since he had completely melted down that day, everybody had been tiptoeing on eggshells around him, as if afraid to set him off once more. In fact, she thought the children were almost relieved to start their new schools, if only to get a little breathing space.

He had been on his best behaviour ever since, of course. All sunshine smiles and terrible Dad jokes, as he had been before. He hadn't so much as snapped at anyone since that night, and the smile he wore seemed permanently sewn to his lips—as if he himself was afraid of what might happen if he allowed it to slip for just one moment.

No one had alluded to the incident. They were

all trying their hardest to believe that it had never happened—that John, the husband and father they had adored, and trusted and relied upon, was not capable of such frightening depths of wrath. That he had not become transformed into a vicious stranger right before their eyes. That he might not do so again, if provoked too far.

But for now, they were all on their best behaviour.

"I'll go pop the kettle on," John murmured. "You go get set up in the studio, if you like."

She gave him a small smile and slipped away, grateful for the reprieve.

Grateful.

The word echoed bitterly around her mind. She had never thought she would be glad to get away from him. When they had first started renting studio spaces together, back in London, all her friends and family had warned her about spending too much time with him.

Living together, working together. It'll be far too much. You'll get sick of the sight of each other, well-meaning acquaintances had said. *It'll only cause arguments.*

But she had known with a rock-solid certainty that it wouldn't. She loved every inch of John and had wanted to be with him as much as she could. And, for all those long years in their cramped London flat, they'd barely said a cross word to each other.

But now...

She shook her head, trying to dislodge that thought. There was no good dwelling on it, that was all.

She sat at the table, staring at the blank sketch book page before her, twiddling a pencil between her fingers. Inspiration was hovering just out of reach, just beyond the tips of her fingers. She could almost see the shadow of what she wanted just lingering there in the murky recesses of her mind, but every time she stretched out for it, it seemed to shrink further out of sight. She rubbed a hand over her eyes with a sigh.

"Feeling blocked?" John asked sympathetically, placing her favourite cup on the table beside her.

She gave him a strained smile. She had stopped work on the shadow sculpture, and John hadn't asked her why. He probably assumed it was just because they were trying to put this whole thing behind them. Maybe that would have been the sensible answer, but it wasn't the *right* one.

I'm not going to continue to reduce that poor fright-

ened woman down to a moment of fear captured and transfixed forever. She deserves more than that. And so do I. I'm going to make her the sculpture she deserves— not one of fear and pain. One of anger. One of strength. One of justice.

If only I knew how to do it.

She sighed again more deeply than ever and glanced over at John. He was also staring at a blank canvas propped up against the easel. He had his palette and oil-knife ready and get smearing fresh colours together ready to apply, but every time he went to do it, he stopped himself. She hadn't seen him this uncertain since his first solo exhibition, all those years ago.

"You could work on one of your commissions instead?" she suggested softly, and he flinched, pulled out of his revery.

He grimaced at her. His painting commissions were the bread and butter that kept the lights on between her larger sales, but he always resented painting to a specification for someone else when he'd far rather be drawing original inspiration from his own creations. Which was why he was so determined to have a gallery of their own, she knew.

And that is something else we haven't mentioned since, his all-consuming desire to own his own art gallery. He used to work it into conversation at least once a day. He hasn't mentioned it at all since that day...

Guilt squirmed in her stomach. She shouldn't have said all that about the gallery. She didn't mind sacrificing to make his dreams a reality. She wanted him to be happy. And if he didn't pursue it just because they'd had an argument, she knew she wouldn't forgive herself. But she was too much of a coward to be the one to bring it up first, all the same. The tentative truce between them was too fragile to be risked in that way.

John huffed.

"I just don't know why I can't do it," he burst out in frustration, casting the palette aside with a clatter.

Abbie couldn't help herself. She flinched at the loud noise.

John did too, a guilty look darting across his face. He gave her a broad grin instead, as if he could cover over the moment. "You're right. I'll do one of the commissions. If you try too hard to find inspiration, it runs away from you. I've always said that."

He whistled a little too loudly as he went to fetch up his half-finished piece instead.

They worked silently side by side for the rest of the day, but she wasn't sure that either of them were really very productive. John finished up one of his commissions and left it to one side to dry, ready for postage, but his eyes kept drifting back to the blank canvas on the easel every five minutes and she was sure his heart wasn't really in it. As for her, her sketch pad remained as defiantly blank as it had done this morning.

At last, she had to concede defeat.

"I'll go pick up the kids," she murmured as she got to her feet. "I'll pop into the village after school too to pick up some groceries, so I'll be a little while."

"Righto," John said distantly, still staring blankly at the empty canvas on the easel.

She hesitated in the hallway, casting a guilty glance back towards the studio, but John was still fully immersed in his daydreams. Scarcely daring to breathe, she crept up to the bedroom, retrieved her hidden box and slipped out of the front door once more, whispering it shut silently.

She could feel her secret treasure beside her on the passenger seat all the way across the narrow winding roads that led to Max's school. As she parked up on the road outside, she all but snatched it from its box.

The broken mirror glinted back at her and all her

breath rushed out of her at once. It was addictive, that was for sure. Dangerously so, perhaps, but she couldn't have given it up for anything now. It sometimes felt like she was only really herself when she was staring into the shards—as if nothing except this moment was quite real, somehow.

Without a flicker of hesitation, she used the jagged tip of one of the fragments to put a pinprick in her thumb, and allowed the tiny dab of blood which flowed out to smear across the shiny surface.

Shadows moved beneath the pinkish smudge. She leant forwards, captivated as always.

The shapes were hard to make out, small as they were, but they were more fascinating than any tv show. There was a humdrum realness to them that fixated her. An old woman in an old fashioned, shapeless dress and plain woollen shawl sat at a wooden bench, cutting up herbs. A kerchief was tied around her neck and a stained apron was fastened around her waist. A small black cat was curled up on the rocking chair by the fire behind her, one that seemed oddly familiar, though Abbie couldn't quite have said why. She'd never had a cat of her own. A girl—probably around Sophie's age—sat at the table too, in a far neater gown, with a bodice and a tailored fit. Her face seemed paler than the weather-beaten woman's beside her, and her hair had a vivid auburn hue to it, though perhaps that was accentuated by the tint of blood Abbie was peering through. She was writing in a leather-bound book and chattering merrily as she did so. Abbie would have given her left arm to hear them too, but no sounds ever came drifting out of the mirror. The pair within laughed merrily at some jape Abbie couldn't hear, the young girl grinning broadly, but the older woman throwing back her head to the ceiling and cackling like a crow.

They look happy...

She didn't know why the thought was so wistful. Quite often when she spied on them, they were. Sometimes the old woman was alone, pottering around her house, carding wool or cutting herbs or stewing poultices over the pot on the fire. Several times that girl had been there though. She was probably a relative of some kind, Abbie guessed—a granddaughter or a niece, perhaps, or maybe just a friendly neighbour. Occasionally other women were there too, sometimes heavily pregnant, sometimes limping along with some ailment or other for the old lady to fix. She never had any men visitors, or not that Abbie had noticed anyway. But the old lady always seemed busy and contented. She had a happy little life which Abbie clung to vicariously.

But the happiness was soon shattered. Even as Abbie watched, the door of the small hut before her was flung open. She watched both women yelping silently as a balding middle-aged man barged his way in, red-faced and shouting. He flung the contents of the table to the floor with one sweep of his arm, fastened his hand tightly around the girl's wrist and hauled her away again, still bellowing out vicious curses Abbie couldn't hear.

Fury flooded Abbie as she watched the old woman slump to the table in dejection. She wished she could reach through the broken glass to the woman who was now resting her head on her arms on the tabletop, but the woman wasn't even aware that Abbie was here, a voyeur to her life. Slowly, the woman picked up the scattered ingredients and gathered them once more. Her bowl was smashed though, so she picked up the pieces and went to the front door to discard them.

Abbie let out a little gasp. She held the mirror right up to her eye, squinting hard. Yes! There, through the sunlight streaming through the open doorway, was a familiar hill and dell—and there, in the slip of the slope sat the mill itself. Even through the mirror and centuries separating them, the little surface of the millpond seemed dark and malevolent—out of place, somehow, as if the way she was seeing it now wasn't quite how it really was.

The waters there are somehow out of time, I think. They're the source of this darkness, I know it.

She shuddered.

With a sudden, decisive nod, the old woman was suddenly striding towards Abbie herself—or, at least, towards the little mirror propped up on the mantlepiece, Abbie belatedly realised. The old woman took a deep breath, her eyes fluttering shut—and when she opened them again, she was looking directly at Abbie. Not just at her own reflection, not just staring into space—but right at Abbie herself! Their eyes met across the span of years and they both flinched, but neither of them ran.

"I'm trying to help you," Abbie murmured, wishing futilely that the old woman could hear and understand her. "I know something awful has happened to you—or will happen to you—but I'm not going anywhere. I'm going to try to help."

The old woman's brow crinkled slightly in confusion, staring at Abbie's lips as if she could decipher the words there. Slowly, she nodded, not as though she understood it, Abbie thought, just as if she recognised Abbie as a fellow woman, a well-wisher—an inevitable part of her future that she could not outrun, even if she wished to.

I think she's one of the bravest people I've ever met. I cannot let her down.

The trill of the alarm on her phone made her startle, and with one last rueful smile at the old lady, Abbie hastily hid the mirror away and clambered out to collect Max.

He was in a good mood today, but Abbie struggled to concentrate on it. As he buckled himself in and she navigated the car over to the secondary school to pick up Sophie, he was busy chattering away about his latest school project. It was some self-directed learning thing that John probably would be pleased about, but which Sophie privately thought was just a way for the teachers to catch up on all their paperwork before the Christmas holidays.

"So, you can take me to the county council offices, can't you, Mum?"

"Well, probably," she said. "But I'm not sure they'll have what you're looking for. If you're doing this family tree project, all our relatives will be in London, won't they?"

"Mrs Roberts said," he began hotly, and Abbie

hastily agreed before the argument spiralled any further out of control, silently cursing Mrs Roberts. Max had always taken instructions too literally.

"Well, we can check," she said. "I think your dad wanted to check out more about the history of the old mill anyway, so he can make a plaque for the new gallery if we ever build it. I'm sure he can take you, and that'll kill two birds with one stone."

She pulled into the carpark and waved at Sophie, who was lounging against the wall with a gaggle of girls. Her friends were all giggling, but Sophie just smiled, a little pale, and a little tired looking.

Abbie's heart lurched. Sophie hadn't been complaining much lately, but it had clearly been a lot for her.

It's only a few more weeks until the school holidays. Then we can all have a lie in and a catch up.

"Bye, Ellie," her friends called as Sophie sloped over and clambered into the back seat beside Max.

"Ellie? Who's Ellie?" Max asked.

Sophie went a burning red. "It's just something I'm trying. I dunno. Dad said the good thing about a new school was you could reinvent yourself, if you wanted to. Just thought I'd try it, is all."

"You can't just change your name!" Max spluttered.

"Why does it matter to you?" Sophie snapped back.

"Alright, alright, both of you, that's enough. Max, if she wants to reinvent herself, she's allowed to. That's what your teenage years are for. Sophie, try not to lose your temper. Or—wait, do you want us to call you Ellie too?"

Sophie went redder than ever, slumping down so low in the seat that Abbie could barely see the top of her head in the rear-view mirror. "Whatever. I don't care. It doesn't matter."

Abbie bit back a sigh as she indicated and pulled away again. Beneath the passenger seat beside her, she could almost feel the weight of that box, and the glass it hid. She wondered if, years away, the old woman was still frowning into her own mirror, entranced by a stranger's face staring right back at her.

Abbie sent Max and Sophie in with the shopping bags when they got home, whilst she flitted up the stairs with her hidden treasure once more. She longed to take just one peek at it to see if the old woman was still there, to see if they could still see each other through the glass—but she knew better than to risk it. John had been temperamental lately, and he had been insistent that they leave everything magical and mystical about this mill behind them. He would fly off the handle completely if he knew she was performing magic herself...

If that is what this is, of course.

She didn't know what else to call it. It wasn't the bubbling cauldrons and sparkly lights sort of thing she'd always associated with magic, or the stripy tights, cackling, Halloween-esque sort of craft one pictured when you said witchcraft, but it clearly wasn't *normal* either.

Well, after all, what is normal? She thought, almost crossly, as she set about preparing dinner and the children squabbled loudly over the TV remote. *Just because we don't fully understand something, doesn't make it wrong, does it?*

Still, she didn't think she'd mention it to John all the same, just as she wouldn't mention the invisible feline presence hissing and spitting around the house at odd moments. He was still staring at the blank canvas in his easel when she called him in for dinner, he drifted back to it as soon as dinner was over, and he was still there a few hours later as she ushered the kids up to their bedrooms to get ready for bed.

He hated being creatively blocked, she knew. It always picked away at him, something that he couldn't just leave alone. She was half tempted to go and throw any old paint on that canvas for him, just to take away its intimidatingly stark whiteness, and a few months ago, maybe she would have. But she couldn't depend on what sort of reaction she'd get now, if she did.

Surreptitiously, she peeked into the mirror under the bed after she'd checked that the kids had done their teeth, but it remained stubbornly empty this time, no matter how much blood she smeared across it.

She saw me. She knew I was watching her. Maybe she took some precautions to stop me peeking?

Or maybe someone else has...

That thought sent a shiver down her spine and she shoved the glass away, taking the stairs three at a time back down to the warmth and glow of the lower rooms, as if she could outrun her own fears.

John had abandoned his futile attempts at painting at last. He was watching nonsense on the telly in the living room, but he turned it off as she approached, and she collapsed onto the sofa with a sigh.

"Children are both down," she said as she snuggled into his side, and he slipped his arm over her shoulder. "Max is asleep already—he needs you to take him to the local county offices at the weekend for some school project—and Sophie is reading in her room. That's one good thing about the move, she seems to have rediscovered her love of reading."

He looked at her sharply. "Reading what?"

"Oh, I don't know. A book from the school library, I guess."

He nodded, relaxing slightly, and smiled. "That's good, then. I knew she had a brain in there somewhere."

"She's a very bright girl," Abbie said warmly. "And she's empathetic and kind. She's just a teenager. You must remember what it was like. I wouldn't go back to those years if you paid me to." She grinned as a memory resurfaced. "I remember trying to reinvent myself too. I tried out 'Gail' instead of 'Abbie' for a week or two, but it didn't stick. I suspect Sophie will be back to 'Sophie' again in a few weeks," she added.

John glanced down at raising an eyebrow. "What's that?"

"Oh, didn't I tell you? She's trying out new personalities at school. Asked all her friends to call her Ally, or Ellie, or something."

"Ellie?" John asked with a small smile. "That's —" But then his expression froze. She could feel his muscles stiffening beneath her.

"John, what's wrong?"

But he had already dislodged her, thundering up the stairs, calling Sophie's name. Abbie flew after him, her heart in her throat.

"What's all this now?" he demanded, barging into her room, making Sophie yelp. There was no book in her hands now, Abbie noticed. She must have hidden it when she heard him stomping up the stairs, and no wonder, for he'd probably be furious if it wasn't precisely the right sort of book he wanted these days. "You think you're called Beth now, do you? Where did you get that from? That wretched grimoire?"

"It's not a grimoire! I didn't—I just—," tears had sprung to Sophie's eyes, and her cheeks were a burning red.

"Stop it, John!" Abbie yelled, tugging him away. "You're scaring her. What does it matter what she calls herself? You were always supportive of the children's self-expression before! What's got into you? You're becoming someone totally different!"

He glowered at her and then froze. He licked his

lips, and shook her gently off, loosening his muscles with a small shrug.

"Sorry," he muttered. "You're right. That was a massive over-reaction."

"You think?" Abbie screeched, her tempers refusing to be assuaged so easily. "John, we can't keep living like this!"

Panic flared through his face. "What the hell does that mean?"

Abbie crossed the room, pulling Sophie into her arms. Her daughter clung to her, shivering, staring wide-eyed at her father. "You can't keep doing this to us, John. We can't live never knowing what is going to set you off next. You need to see someone— an anger management counsellor, or a shrink or something."

He ran a hand over his face, his skin hollow and grey. He staggered as though he had been hit and slumped against the wall, sliding down it until he had pooled at the bottom.

"There's something I need to tell you," he said hoarsely. "I didn't tell you before because I didn't want to admit, even to myself, that there was a possibility of..." He shook his head, blew out a wavering breath and tried again. "That book we found in the hidden room," he said. "It belonged to an old lady called Catrin Waterhouse. She's a bit of a local legend around here, apparently, the last woman to be killed as a witch in the area. She was drowned in our millpond and the locals say that she cursed it as she died. I thought that if you knew, you might panic. You might think your shadow woman —all the strange things that have been happening— you might..." He looked at her helplessly and then turned his gaze towards Sophie instead. "But Catrin was just a herb wife. She didn't have the knowledge of reading and writing, so she got one of the local girls to do it for her. A girl called Beth Miller. When you started calling yourself that too, I thought, I don't know, I just..."

Beth.

The vision of the girl through the mirror sprang to Abbie's eyes once more. The laughing, well-dressed girl scribbling down notes, who had flinched as that man came bursting in to drag her away, already expecting the violence before it descended.

Which must make the older woman Catrin.

Something in Abbie shifted. The whole mad dream seemed far more real now there was a name attached.

"Please," John said hoarsely, flinching her out of

her reflections. "Please. I know it's silly superstition, but I just don't think we should be messing around with this stuff. I'm... I'm *scared*."

Abbie's heart lurched towards him. John was never scared of anything. It was the optimist in him. He never thought there was anything that they couldn't somehow survive, or work through, or turn to their advantage.

She crossed to him and wrapped her arms around him tightly. "We're going to be alright," she promised.

"Don't leave me, Abs," he whispered, burying his face in her neck. "I know I've been... I'm sorry. I'm trying to control it. I just... please... I'll see someone. I'll get help."

Abbie nodded firmly.

And so will I, she thought fiercely—already returning in her mind to the one person who might be able to solve this whole mess, waiting for her on the other side of a cracked and broken mirror.

CHAPTER 7
THE RISING WATERS

*C*atrin Waterhouse. Beth Miller.

Abbie clung to those two names fiercely all the way to the local county offices. They'd decided to make it a family trip, in the end, because it was attached to the local library and Sophie wanted to get a new book out. John was going to help Max with his genealogy project and look up the history of the mill, but Abbie was going to find out as much as she could about Catrin and Beth. She couldn't stop those wicked men from drowning Catrin, of course, she was about four hundred years too late for that, but she could still *help* her, of that she was certain. She had to be able to, or all of this would be for nothing.

The archivist behind the desk was less than helpful though. "There's plenty of books on Catrin Waterhouse in the library," he said, pointing down the corridor. "You'll more likely find what you're looking for there, than here."

But Abbie didn't need second-hand stories of supposed legends. She didn't need to hear how the villagers had woven their fairytales around a poor, lonely old woman and murdered her for their own ends. How they had accused her of a darkness they themselves harboured and made her the scapegoat. She needed *facts*. When she was born. The date that she died. Who she had lived amongst, whether Beth Miller, the girl she had died to save, had survived. Whether she had married and had children. Whether any of Catrin's sacrifices had been *worth* it.

"Well, you can check the records," the archivist said doubtfully. "I'm not sure how much good it will be though."

But as Abbie was led to a computer where the digitised files were displayed, she found someone already there waiting for her.

"Mr Edwards! What are you doing here?"

He gestured at the old, bulky computer before him. "Just a bit of genealogy. You start to take an interest in that kind of thing at my age. When there's not so much time for you to look forward to, it's natural to take a look back, I reckon. I've got back as far as the 18th century, so far, but I'm still plugging away at it." He looked her over shrewdly and then added, "You'll be here looking for the truth of our Catrin, I take it. I wondered when you might come."

She hesitated and then nodded. He gestured to the seat by the computer beside him, and she slipped into it.

"You've seen her, haven't you, in the water?" he guessed. "The women always do. I don't know why she never shows herself to men. You'd think she'd be angrier at the men, not the women."

"She's not angry." The words came blurting out before she could stop them.

Mr Edwards raised an eyebrow at her. "Not angry? She's placed a powerful curse on this village for centuries, and she's not angry?"

"I don't... I don't think it's from her," she said slowly, not really sure what she meant even as she said it. "It's just a feeling. But she feels *afraid*. I think that's why she only shows herself to women. She's trying to warn us away. I think she's trying to protect us..."

Mr Edwards scratched a gnarled hand over his

blue veined chin. "Could be, could be. Funny way of doing it though, to my mind, luring folks into the same pool that drowned her. That sounds like revenge to me."

Abbie leant forwards; her eyes fixed on his face. "Tell me everything," she said.

Mr Edwards chuckled. "Don't know about *everything*, but I'll tell you the story as I heard it as a boy. The way the legend goes is that Catrin Waterhouse was a local herb witch and midwife, helping out the local women with their births and their ailments and the like, just as she had done all her life. And no one thought a thing of it, until she started befriending the miller's girl."

"Beth Miller," Abbie put in.

Mr Edwards nodded. "Well, milling was a profitable business during those days, and Beth was an only child. She was one of the richest people in the village and educated to match. But when her father died, her uncle came and took his place. Beth turned overnight from a happy heiress to a withdrawn loner, until she started to hang about with old Catrin Waterhouse that is. Well, the new miller was none too happy about that. Said Catrin was not appropriate company for a woman of Beth's standing and there were to have no more to do with each other."

"But they didn't listen," Abbie guessed. "They were friends. They needed each other. They still saw each other in secret."

"Right you are," Mr Edwards agreed. He waggled a finger at her. "Until things started going wrong around the village, that is. The well was spoilt, the apple stores turned, sheep were born with disfigurements. The sort of thing which does happen in a little rural village from time to time, of course, but the new miller leapt on it. Sent off for a witchfinder general and one came. A new one, eager to make his name. Matthew ." He leant forwards, holding her gaze. "Well, this accuses *both* women of witchcraft, Catrin and Beth both."

"Because they found the herb book?" Abbie guessed, but Mr Edwards was shaking his head now.

"Don't know nothing about any herb book. But Catrin had a mirror—an expensive little thing it would have been, far beyond the pocketbook of a midwife. The new miller said she had stolen it from him for scrying, but Beth said she had gifted it to Catrin as a thank you for some healing she had done, and that sealed both their fates. Beth was accused of being a witch's apprentice and Catrin was accused of seducing her into the dark arts and unnatural relations with the devil himself." He leant forwards lowering his voice. "Scandalous rumours, and probably nothing more, but it was enough to damn her."

"Did they drown them both then?" Abbie whispered, her eyes wide, horror curling through her stomach. Beth had been so young in the mirror—just Sophie's age—she had had her whole life ahead of her.

"No, for Catrin took the blame, you see," Mr Edwards said. "She confessed to stealing the mirror and even to witchcraft and unnatural conversation with the devil, but says that Beth never had a thing to do with it. She said that young Beth Miller had been under her enchantments and was utterly and completely innocent of all wrongdoing, so the story goes. Beth was spared and Catrin was drowned in the miller's pond."

"Oh, how tragic," Abbie breathed, her hands fleeing to her lips as she blinked back tears. "She was so brave."

Mr Edwards nodded. "But that's not the end of it, you see. That night, both the miller and the witchfinder general died, and Beth disappeared forever, leaving Anglesey never to return. And ever since then, well, the millpond has been cursed. Anyone who gets too close to it, finds themselves oddly affected. Accidents happen. Strange dreams and visions, strange voices. And sooner or later, they all end up in the pool too. Three drownings there have been in that pool in my lifetime, and I've only been on this earth, what, seventy-six years now? Who knows how many more there were before my time?"

He reached across the table, his hand fastening around her wrist with a surprising strength, just as he had done back outside the café all those weeks ago. "Don't be next," he whispered. "And don't let your little girl be next neither."

Abbie nodded and thanked him for his time, rising to go. His warnings echoed through her mind as she wandered through the tall, overladen shelves to find the others, but she didn't believe it all the same. There was danger in the millpond. There was even death. But she did not—could not—believe that the same woman who laughed and joked with a young, lonely girl and who confessed to a crime she did not commit just to spare her friend's life, could be responsible for so much hate and violence after her death.

She just needs help, she thought again. *And I am not going to be frightened away this time.*

As suspected, the local county office had not been very much use at all for Max's genealogy project. He had somehow persuaded the archivist there to write a short note to Mrs Roberts explaining that he had, in fact, been as she had told him to though, so he was pacified for now, at least. Sophie was reading her new book in the back of the car, *A practical guide to lapidary medicine,* which sounded official and medical enough to trick John, at least. He hadn't appeared to notice yet that it was a guide to crystal healing, and he would surely be utterly scathing when he did see, but it was an argument for another time.

John himself was quiet and distracted all the way home.

"What's wrong?" she murmured at him.

He glanced over at her, then peeked into the rear-view mirror to check that the children were both distracted. "I researched the history of that mill," he murmured in an undertone, low enough that they couldn't hear. "It's bizarre, Abs. It seems to go in these weird cycles."

"What do you mean?"

He glanced into the back again, but neither of the children were eavesdropping. "Every decade or two, someone new takes the mill. There's always an accident, or a flood, or a violent murder—"

"Murder?" Abbie repeated, far too loudly.

John hushed her, but the children had both looked up.

"What's that, Mum?" Max asked.

"We're just discussing a TV programme from last night," she said hastily. "I missed the ending and your Dad was filling me in."

Both children turned back to their own distractions, instantly bored.

Abbie grimaced an apology over to John, whose hands had gone very white against the steering wheel. Her stomach was churning uneasily.

*John would never murder us. Of course he wouldn't. Even if the aura did infect him and make him angrier than ever, he'd **never** deliberately hurt us...*

But she couldn't help looking at him in a new way, all the same, and the memory of the jam jar shattering against the wall replayed over and over in her mind.

He shrugged. "People die," he murmured. "Or they're seriously injured and they run away before something worse happens. And then the mill sits empty for another ten to twenty years, until someone new comes along, and it all starts up once more."

The push and pull, she thought distantly, *just like Cerys said before. The aura of this house is so confused. It wants to drag us in and kill us, and it wants to send us away at the same time...*

She ran her hands through her bobbed hair, her stomach somersaulting.

"What about you? What did you find out?" he muttered.

She filled him in on everything Mr Edwards had said in an undertone.

He nodded grimly. "That fits with what Nicole and Richard said at the heritage centre," he mumbled. "They said—"

But what they said, she was never destined to find out. As John navigated the car through the gate and down the driveway, he cursed softly, slamming on the brakes hard enough to make them all lurch against their seatbelts.

Water, black and murky, spilled up the driveway towards them, bursting over the banks of the millpond. It was lapping up against the walls of the house and had probably flooded right the way inside whilst they were gone this afternoon.

Whatever is in that millpond is coming for us now. It's not content to wait to lure us into the waters any longer. It's hunting us out itself.

"Everything will be ruined," John whispered. "All the furniture, all the woodwork, everything. It hasn't even been raining today! How has this happened? Has a pipe burst somewhere, or something?"

He glanced over at Abbie. "You're not saying anything?" he snapped. "I thought you'd be panicking by now."

She still didn't reply, staring out across the water rippling malevolently up towards them. It seemed almost smug somehow, she thought. A fine mist had descended over the surface of the waters, so thick that she couldn't see the other side of it. Even from inside the car, she could hear the churn and clunk of the waterwheel twisting with a dreadful slowness through the still waters. The afternoon light bounced strangely off the mist, making the shadows of the trees all around them move and dance, like a baying mob hemming them in, coming for them.

John shifted in his seat and glanced back at the

kids in the back. "You're not frightened either?" he demanded, almost crossly, as if they ought to be.

Sophie shrugged wearily, only glancing up briefly from her book. "I was expecting it. I dreamed the pond flooded last night."

He opened his mouth angrily at that, but Abbie lay a restraining hand on his wrist. His hand was burning hot, as if he were aflame. He glared at her, and then caught himself, blowing out a slow breath as he shook her off. "Right. Well. As long as everyone's OK. That's the main thing. Insurance can sort out the rest, I suppose. I'll ring them now."

Poor John. He so desperately needs to believe there's no magic in it. He always has been a sceptic.

She gave him a small smile as he clambered out of the car and began striding around wrangling people on the end of the phone. His shadow joined the others in the mist, lurching out before him monstrously, pacing the floor. He waved his arms wildly as he ranted, and she could almost picture the pitchfork in it, ready to attack. She turned away.

"You're both alright?" she asked the others far too brightly. "The waters don't look too deep. I imagine your bedrooms will be fine, I don't think the flooding has gone to the upper floors, though perhaps the TV in the living room might not have survived."

Max had an odd expression on his face, one she couldn't quite read. "What is it, Max? What's the matter?"

He glanced at her then, and she startled away. He didn't look angry or afraid, she realised. He looked *satisfied.*

"You're pleased the pond flooded!" she said. She could hear the note of accusation in her voice and she tried to wipe it away, but she couldn't. She forced a grin. "You think you can get out of school for a day or two, perhaps?"

"Max likes school," Sophie pointed out, still reading her book.

"It's not that, Mum. It's just right, isn't it? Every action has a consequence. The consequence of messing with the millpond is that it messes right back with you," he said matter-of-factly. "If you dabble in darkness, it will claim you. That's only natural."

Dabble in darkness?

These were not her little boy's words. He had always come out with weird sayings far too old for his tender years, of course, but he'd never had any interest in the occult or spiritual before. To hear him parroting these things so calmly was far more unnerving even than John's sudden rages.

Not my babies. You can taunt me and torment John if you must, we're adults, we can take it, but you will leave Sophie and Max out of it, she vowed silently.

But the car door swung open again before she could reply. The smell of cold water and stale air rushed in with it, filling the car, choking her. John didn't seem to notice.

"They're putting us up in a hotel for the night and sending someone around to sort it out," he said, just a tad brusquely, as he strapped himself in. "I'll drive you over there now and then I'll come back to help. I'll pack a bag for us when I return, but they said they'd only put us up for one night, so not to get too comfortable." He snorted scornfully. "Remind me what we pay our insurance bills for again?"

Abbie smiled weakly, settling herself back against the seat, but her eyes kept to Max in the rearview mirror, all the same. The gleeful satisfaction on his face sent shivers over her skin as they pulled out once more. The creaking screech of the waterwheel behind them echoed in her mind as John drove away far too fast, fleeing from the rising waters and the lingering stench of self-righteousness as though they were being chased.

THE HOTEL only had one room spare, so all four of the Harpers crammed in together, John and Abbie on the double bed, Sophie and Max on cot beds on the floor.

The back rooms and upper rooms of their house had escaped the worst of the damage, but the living room and hall were utterly ruined. The insurance people were just as mystified as John as to how it had happened, but they had summoned the flood restoration service to pump out the stale water and drain the millpond a little, and they had put plans in place to return when it was drier to erect sturdier flood defences. They had also agreed to reimburse the cost of replacing the floorboards, skirting boards and electrical goods in the front room and hall—so who knew how much their premiums would go up now, but John supposed that it couldn't be helped.

I'll just have to take on some more commissions to cover the cost, that's all. And if Abbie ever gets a move on with a new sculpture, that would help.

He felt a wave of anger cresting over him them that he couldn't quite explain. He closed his eyes, wiping it away with trembling hands.

Nine murders in the past four hundred years. The

records he had looked at today had been nauseatingly grim. Of the past twenty occupiers of the mill and adjourning mill house, almost half of them had ended up killing their loved ones, either accidentally or on purpose. Time and again he had read about it in the newspaper archives. Men holding their wives, lovers and daughters under the water until they drowned. Pushing them in. Forcing their heads beneath the waves as they struggled and thrashed, women they were supposed to have loved and protected. And none of them had really been able to explain why they had done it. It seemed an odd coincidence that it was always women murdered too. Surely at least some of that historic violence should be aimed at other men or boys? Perhaps, in the eyes of a cowardly murderer, it was just easier to take out their wrath on innocent women?

John shuddered.

I cannot become that man.

Even the thought of it was repellent, twisting in his stomach. The sight of Abbie and Sophie floating face down in the millpond kept creeping into his mind and as much as he wanted to, he couldn't push it away.

He glanced at Abbie beside him in the bed. She was damp and twitching, as if the floodwaters had followed her here. She wasn't the only one. Sophie, down on the floor, kept yelping too, kicking and thrashing through her dreams, trying to ward off imaginary attackers.

He watched her silently for a moment.

There's a taint of magic in her now. It's too late for her. She's beyond salvation.

Sophie woke with a gasp as if she had heard him. She scrabbled up the bed in seconds, kicking the duvet away as violently as if it were an intruder. John was by her inside instantly, all other thoughts abandoned.

"You're alright, Soph. You're safe. More nightmares?" he guessed in a whisper.

She just gave him an odd look he couldn't decipher.

"You won't be in trouble," he promised, his insides squirming. "I never should have said you couldn't tell me about them. I'm sorry."

"They're not nightmares, I think. They're memories," Sophie whispered, her eyes hollow and haunted. "He hates himself almost as much as he hates her, but he won't stay away. She'd kill him if she could, but she's afraid of being caught. She doesn't want to hang. She doesn't want to die."

"Catrin?"

"Beth," she breathed, tucking her knees up to her chest and burying her head in them, as if she could fold herself up pocket-small and protect herself that way. Her next words came out muffled and blurred. "I can still feel her fear and her anger, Dad. It's all so vivid. They think I'm her. They keep calling out to me. They won't leave me alone."

"But you know that you're not her, right?" John said anxiously. "That's not why you started to call yourself Ellie, is it? You do remember who you really are?"

Sophie didn't say anything at all, and a shiver ran over John's skin.

We never should have come here at all. We should have stayed in London where we were safe. Abbie was right.

Behind them, as if summoned by his thoughts, Abbie also awoke, gasping for breath.

"Not you too," John groaned.

Abbie just blinked at him. She didn't seem scared, like Soph. She just seemed resigned and exhausted.

"Tell me, then," he demanded hoarsely, but Abbie had already settled back against the pillows.

"Same as every night," she murmured sleepily,

half-asleep again already. "Drowning. Always drowning. In the millpond."

Every night? Why didn't she say something earlier?

But John already knew the answer to that, of course. He had told her not to.

He sat back, staring between his wife and his daughter.

"Alright," he said at last. "I don't think I can fight this any longer. I—I'll admit that there's something... *unusual* going on here. Something we can't explain away with logic." He grimaced, then his jaw tightened. "So, what are we going to do about it? I'm not just going to sit idly by whilst my wife and daughter get haunted to death."

And I'm not going to be the one to kill them, he promised himself silently.

To his surprise, Abbie laughed then, her face creasing softly into a tender expression. "Oh, John. I've missed you."

"I've been doing some reading," Sophie said quietly. "I think Catrin is trapped."

"Trapped? She's dead!" John said.

Sophie rolled her eyes, just as she always used to, and he had never been gladder to see it.

"No, her spirit is trapped, Dad. There was some dark magic in it. I think the same spell which killed the miller and the witchfinder general also trapped Catrin."

"But Catrin was already dead when those men died," Abbie said slowly. "Even if she was a witch, could she have cursed them from beyond the grave?"

"I don't know. There's a bit about hexes and how to break them in the back of Catrin's book, but I haven't got to that bit yet." She glanced at her dad guiltily.

John frowned. "The book is still with the museum. They were going to send it off for testing to see if it was authentic or not."

Sophie shook her head. "No. It's in my room."

John choked, gaping at her. "But that's impossible. I handed it over to the heritage centre people myself. They must have security and stuff on it, and if it had gone missing, they'd surely come to check with us first."

Sophie just shrugged. "I don't know what to tell you, Dad. You took it away and when I came back from school it was waiting for me on my pillow again."

"Impossible," he breathed, but Abbie just shrugged.

"Is it so very much more impossible than anything else that's happened lately?" she asked wryly. "And if the heritage centre people think it's away being tested, maybe they haven't noticed it's missing yet anyway. When we get back to the house tomorrow, you can look it up, Soph. The waters didn't rise as far as your bedrooms, so the journal should still be alright. And I think I'll ask Cerys if she has any ideas. She's interested in the occult. She might know a bit about breaking hexes and the like. I think I'll reach out to Mari and Mr Edwards too," she added.

"What? Why? Can't we keep this in the family?" John asked, staring over at her.

He might, begrudgingly, be about to accept that something supernatural was happening here, but that didn't mean he want the rest of the world to know he was accepting this madness too. He didn't want to get a reputation as a madman when they'd only just moved here.

But Abbie shook her head. "Catrin's murder was instigated and condoned by the whole community," she said. "If we're going to stop this all now, I think we're going to need the community to come together and undo what the first villagers did. It's symbolic."

John chewed his lip, his stomach lurching uneasily.

And yet, for Abbie and Sophie's sake, I think we might have to.

He nodded. "Alright," he said tersely. "Let's do it."

~

John dropped Abbie back to the house early the next day before he took the kids to school. The whole house stank of rotting wood and damp, the floorboards warped and peeling, but the waters had sullenly retreated to the millpond by now, and the mist there seemed to have lifted once more. For now, at least, it was quiet.

She found Catrin's book under Sophie's pillow, just where Sophie had said it would be, but Abbie couldn't understand a word of it.

It wasn't meant for me, clearly. The book is Sophie's. The mirror is mine.

She fetched it out from beneath the bed and carried it reverently down to the studio. She didn't need to hide it, anymore, and for that she was glad. She hadn't liked having secrets from John. She pricked her thumb and coated the surface, but Catrin was still hiding from her, it seemed.

"I'm trying to help you," she murmured. "Show me how to do it."

She cast around for inspiration, and her eyes snagged on the sketch she had first made of Catrin's shadow. It was the essence of her lingering spirit, her fear, her desperation. She could almost see the same lady from the mirror in it now, horribly distorted through years of perpetual nightmares. It might help focus her scrying now, she supposed.

She lay the mirror directly on top of the picture and peered down into it. "You don't have to be afraid, Catrin. I'm here."

As if in retort, the shadows swam through the pink. Abbie leant forwards, pressing one eye right up against the glass, scrunching the other tight shut.

Catrin was hobbling around the room, her hands knotting in her apron, her gaze fleeing to the glass-less windows every few seconds. Fear threaded through every rigid inch of her frame. The door thudded open and Catrin leapt out of her skin. Beth, her hair frizzing out of its plait, her skirts dirty and creased, stood framed in the doorway. She was shouting something, though, of course, Abbie could not hear what. She kept pointing over her shoulder, back towards the mill.

Catrin shook her head hard, but Beth was with her, trying to tug her away, pleading with her to flee, Abbie guessed. Catrin glanced at the mirror—at Abbie.

Go, Abbie willed her, even though she knew there was no escape for Catrin now. *Run whilst you can. Escape.*

Catrin scuttled towards the mirror itself, and Abbie flinched as two large hands loomed before her, dragging the mirror off its place on the mantlepiece. The world swam around her as Catrin thrust the mirror at Beth instead, and Abbie's head pounded at the odd new perspective, staring up at the underside of Beth's frightened face. A bag was thrust at Beth too, presumably carrying the tools John had found, and then Catrin shoved her away. Abbie could see her lips moving as she gabbled, trying to make the younger girl run.

Both women turned at once—presumably at some sound Abbie couldn't hear—and then, reluctantly, Beth fled. The world swerved and joggled around her and Abbie only caught confusing glimpses of the undersides of trees and cloud kissed skies—then the back of a bush as Beth crouched, half hidden, watching.

Abbie squinted through the undergrowth too, straining her eyes, wishing she could adjust the mirror for a better look. A crowd of men were marching up to Catrin's little cottage, anger and vicious glee written large on every face. Terror seized every limb, until every part of her ached with the strain of it. Abbie tried to scream a futile warning, but her mouth wouldn't work. She tried to pull away from the mirror—she couldn't watch them kill Catrin, she couldn't bear to—but she couldn't do that either. She was trapped here. Trapped in the glass, forced to watch.

Distantly, she heard the clank of the wheel start up once more, she heard screams rising in a crescendo within her ears, battling the pounding pulse of her heartbeat—she smelt water, rising, could feel it there, around her ankles, climbing up to her knees. She tried to break free.

The world went black.

∼

"Abbie? Abs?" John shook her fiercely. The house had been quiet as he had come in from the school run, but he hadn't thought anything of it until he found her slumped, lifeless across the art table in the studio. She didn't wake, even as he shook her. In her hand was a small, shattered mirror, smeared with faint smudges of pink, clouded with slowly drifting shadows, swirling beyond the fractures.

The inner workings of the water wheel suddenly clunked. John whirled towards them. They scraped against the wall, grinding metal to stone, clanking around with a dreadful inevitability.

Abbie sat up.

"Oh, Abs, you're alright! I was so—"

But Abbie didn't look at him. She stared straight ahead, her gaze unfocused. Her breath hissed out in ragged bursts, but her expression was completely blank, without a flicker of fear or anger in it. He clasped her as she rose. She was icy cold and sodden, as if he'd just pulled her from the bottom of the ocean.

The clanking of the wheel grew louder.

"Abbie, wake up. Wake up!" He tried to hold her. She wrenched herself free with an unnatural strength, her eyes still glassy and vacant. He tried to block the door, but she shoved him aside one handed and walked steadily onwards.

Panicking, he pushed past her, fumbling the

house key into the lock and securing it tightly. Even if this spirit didn't release her, at least she would be safe in the house. She couldn't get into too much trouble here.

But she hauled the door open with a single pull, yanking the lock straight out of the door frame, sending splinters cascading around them.

John held onto her. He could do nothing else. They were pulled together through the squelching earth, onwards, towards that midnight water silently calling her.

That fine mist was back again, thicker than ever. It hung over the surface of the water, obscuring the other side from view. The clacking of the wheel grew even louder. A girl's voice was screaming and, for a moment, John thought it was Sophie, but as he looked around for her, no one was there.

No, the words echoed on the thin drifts of breeze. *No, not Catrin. She's innocent!*

Shadows moved through the mists, a roar of angry voices, and a swell of rage rippled through John in reply. He was burning hot, his skin aflame, as though he had descended into the pits of hell. His vision started to fizz in crackling shades of grey, his tongue coppery and acrid.

"Evil must be purged!" he heard himself screaming. "It must be cut out root and branch. It must not be tolerated, or it will fester and infect every one of us. Purify yourselves, my friends!"

And then, to his horror, John felt his arms moving of their own accord. The fires roared higher. His vision was almost completely black now.

He *shoved* Abbie into the water.

A great cheer ran around the empty yard, a cacophony of voices swelling with gleeful violence —and a high-pitched shriek, veering between pleading for Catrin's life and babbling out revenge, vowing to avenge her.

And, glorious, triumphant, righteous wrath buoyed John, filling him completely.

Abbie's head crested the water, her eyes wide and frightened. The mist vanished. The wheel stopped. John slumped, hollow, frightened and utterly alone.

"Abbie," he gasped hoarsely, fumbling into the water and snatching her up in his arms. She shivered violently, clinging to him. The anger had fled, leaving only panic in its wake.

I cannot become that man. I will not. But I do not know how to stop myself either.

"Let's go," he gabbled, pulling her as close as he could. "You were right. It's too dangerous here. Let's pack up and leave right now. We'll never come back."

But she pulled herself out of his arms, stumbling for the land, squelching and dripping to the sodden earth below. Fury lined every inch of her face. "No, John. I'm tired of running. I'm tired of being afraid. Catrin needs us. And no self-righteous, bloodthirsty bully is going to stop me." Her eyes blazed, and John took a step back. An echo of that same fearsome thirst for vengeance that had echoed through that distantly screaming voice glowed in her gaze. "This ends now," she vowed.

CHAPTER 8
THE WITCH'S REVENGE

Abbie stared around at the impromptu village meeting, crowded into Mari's café that afternoon. She'd picked up the kids from school and dropped them back at home, asking Soph to watch Max for an hour or so whilst they were at this meeting. Not that he needed much watching, all things told. He'd just be getting on his with homework, or reading a book, or delving deep into his new hobby of genealogy.

They're good kids. Both of them are.

She regarded the few villagers who had come in the end, including Cerys and Mr Edwards, as well as a few she didn't recognise by sight. She'd hoped for more, but it was better than nothing, she supposed, and after all, it had been called at the last minute.

It's symbolic, she reminded herself. *There are enough people here to represent the village...*

She just hoped that was true.

John squeezed her hand under the sticky café table. His face was pale and tight. He hadn't said much since they had clambered back out of the pond and changed into warm, dry clothes, but he had stayed by her side the whole time, as though his presence could protect her from the lingering memories haunting their flood-damaged home.

Or, she thought, as though *she* could help protect *him* from the man he feared he was turning into...

She took one last deep breath and got to her feet. The café hushed at once.

"Thank you all for coming at such short notice," she said. Her voice didn't sound like her own anymore. It was oddly stilted and formal. "I suspect many of you have guessed why we asked you here, but let me take a moment to confirm it for you."

She licked her lips, very aware of how insane this would sound when said aloud in the middle of the afternoon in an old café, far away from the rising mists, rippling waters and strange, disembodied voices. But she pushed on anyway. She had to. For Catrin's sake, and for their own.

"The mill is haunted," she said starkly. The

words echoed around the silent room, and every eye stared at her. She could feel a faint blush rising across her cheeks at this ludicrous statement, but she just jutted her chin higher and continued. "We don't know everything, but from what we have managed to discover so far, Catrin Waterhouse was unjustly murdered in the mill pond by a witchfinder general, and her spirit has lingered ever since. It makes the whole area... unsettled. We want to put it to bed once and for all. And we think we're going to need your help to do it. What the village did, the village must undo."

The others looked at each other uneasily.

"I'm not saying you're wrong," Cerys began. "In fact, I think you're probably right, this has been going on far too long, but do you know *how* we could do that? I've tried putting salts and crystals down, it hasn't done much good. I don't know what else we could do now."

"We've found some old artefacts of Catrin's. Some witchcraft tools, an old scrying mirror and her journal. Sophie, my daughter, is reading her way through the journal, searching for clues for how to break hexes. We think that might help."

Mari raised her eyebrows. "You've found Catrin's things?" She glanced at the others, her expression thunderstruck. "That mill must have been renovated a dozen times since Catrin died. How are you only finding them now?"

Cerys folded her arms. "Maybe they were meant to find it then. Maybe it's a sign. It's time, at last." She looked at Abbie and nodded resolutely. "Alright, *cariad*. What do you need us to do?"

～

SOPHIE FROWNED SLIGHTLY at the journal before her as she perched, cross legged, on her bed. The whole house stank of damp now and it was giving her a bit of a headache, which wasn't helping her concentrate. Beth's handwriting was getting more erratic, the scrawls of the cursive slant dashing over half the page, as if she was scribbling it out in a frenzy.

He has traversed nigh upon half the village girls already, Sophie read, *delighting in their fear and the power he holds over them, to accuse or acquit as best pleases his whims. We have thus far avoided his gaze, but it will not be long before he seeks us out and ever my uncle parades our names before him, seeking to accuse us for his own ends. They are looking for a scapegoat and we are truly useful unto that end. I have tried to persuade Catrin to strike first, but she is chary and unwilling to sully her soul. As for me, I do not fear the bodkins—*

"Bodkins?" Sophie murmured aloud, pausing. She scanned ahead, but she couldn't tell from context what it might be. She scrabbled her phone out of her pocket, but she'd forgotten to charge it, and the battery had died. She plugged it in immediately, of course, but it would take a few moments to restart, and she was too impatient to wait. Tension crackled in the musty air of the mill house now, as if a storm was brewing all around them. She had the uncanny feeling that time was running out now, that she didn't have any left to waste.

She went to grab her laptop, but it wasn't in her drawer.

Max. It must be. He's always helping himself to my things.

"Max!" she yelled, slamming the door open. He didn't reply. "Where are you? What have you done with my laptop? I told you not come into my room!"

She kicked his bedroom door open and he startled guiltily, sitting on his bed, illuminated by the blue glow of her laptop screen.

She went to snatch it, but he clung on, pushing her away one handed.

She scowled. "Stop that, Max. It's mine! Go use

Mum's if you need one. She never minds you using hers."

He still didn't relinquish the laptop. "Let go, Sophie, you're going to break it! Anyway, Mum has locked the studio. I can't get hers, and I need the internet to do my family tree project."

"Urgh! You're so ridiculous! Your homework doesn't matter, it's just something your teacher invented to shut you up before Christmas. No one else cares about it half as much as you do. I'm trying to do something *real*."

"This matters too!" he said hotly. "I've got all the way back to 1792 now! That's further than anyone else in the class, Mrs Roberts said! And I've learnt such a lot about our family; we had a navy captain as our great uncle, and an engineer who helped design bridges during the Victorian era, and a woman who had fifteen children and *all* of them were boys—"

"And they're all dead, so none of it matters anymore. I'm trying to help people *now*," Sophie shouted.

All dead.

The words echoed through the suddenly silent room. The air thickened between them. Sophie's heartbeat suddenly began to rabbit, though she couldn't have said why. Thin tendrils of creeping mist slowly seeped through the closed windowpane.

With a lethal quiet, Max got to his feet. A malevolent anger she had never seen there before glinted darkly in his eyes. It seemed out of place on a child's face, as if his chubby youthfulness had to contort around it, warping his innocence into bitter maturity.

"Say that again," he hissed, his voice distorting strangely.

Again, distant voices echoed tauntingly. *It's all happening again.*

"Stop it, Max. That's not funny." She tried to make her voice come out firm and authoritative, but it sounded oddly shrill and desperate instead.

He took a step towards her, his feet creaking the floorboards beneath. Though she was far taller than him, instinctively, she took a step back.

"Who do you think you are?" he spat, venom curling through every syllable. "You think you're better than me, do you? Too good for me? I should have got rid of you months ago. You're only here on sufferance."

Sufferance. Those couldn't be Max's words; she doubted he even knew what it meant.

Suffer, the echo chanted back at her gleefully, taking up the call.

Sophie's throat tightened. She took another step backwards and bumped up against the wall. It should have been smooth plaster, but it felt like cold, rough stone there beneath her fingers. "Stop it, Max. This isn't you. You've got to fight it."

Max roared wordlessly, picking up her laptop one-handed and hurling it against the wall. It smashed, the screen fracturing into glowing, fizzing, static lines in the broken black.

Sophie screamed.

"If I can't have it, no one can," he bellowed, his hands bunched at his sides. Veins stood out in thick relief all the way along his arms and neck.

If I can't have you, no one can.

Hands seemed to snatch at Sophie then, though Max, a few feet away, hadn't moved. Invisibly, they grasped at her arms, roamed her waist, seized around her throat, hard enough to bruise. She tried to scream again but couldn't suck enough air down to do it.

Max's face swam before her eyes, contorting with fury. It seemed to change in the mist, warping and bulging oddly until his small nose became large and red-veined and his smooth chin grew broader, bruised with stubble-rash. His hair lengthened and coarsened, peppered with grey, lank with grease, and his eyes, usually so blue and innocent, became red-rimmed, bloodshot and furious.

Her vision swam until it seemed as if she were in two rooms at once—one neat, warm, and bright with a furious ten-year-old opposite her, the other dark, cold and stone-clad, a middle-aged man pressing up hard against her, louring down at her. His hands, large and square with blunt, dirty nails, tightened further around her throat, making her gasp and squirm.

He's already killed her. Now he's going to kill me too, just like he always threatened to.

The voice seemed to swim out of the back of her mind, and in her muddled state, she wasn't quite sure it belonged to her.

The mist grew thicker still.

"You saw what happened to your old friend tonight," he leered, flecks of spittle dripping from his cracked lips. "She saved you this time, but she's not here to save you anymore, is she?"

Sophie tried to kick him away, but her legs became tangled in her thick woollen skirts.

Skirts? I was wearing jeans.

He rammed her up against the stonework. The

shutters beside her rattled in the glassless windows as the starlit night outside swept in.

"Uncle," she heard herself choking out. "Don't."

"If you don't want to go the same way, you'd best start behaving, hadn't you? Filthy slattern."

He snatched at her apron and ripped it loose, but she snagged it in her trembling fingers as it fell. As he began fumbling at her neck-kerchief, yanking at her dress, and anger, hotter than any she had felt before, filled her.

Catrin had been *good*. She alone, of all the village, had tried to help Beth, had tried to protect her. A crime her uncle had deemed worthy of death, apparently.

Beth—Sophie—stretched the apron strings tight in her calloused hands.

"Catrin didn't deserve to die," she choked out. "*You* do."

His eyes went wide with surprise as the apron strings tightened around his bulging throat. It bit deep as she twisted it, choking off the air, yanking it with all her strength until the stitching began to fray and threatened to snap entirely. His face went red—then purple. His large meaty paws scrambled for his throat, clawing futilely for air, but she was relentless. Vengeance poured through her. She was justice. Retribution. An avenging angel.

Not Max, Sophie screamed distantly in the back of her mind. *Max is an innocent. He doesn't deserve to get tangled up in this.*

As if she had heard, Beth's hands loosened slightly, but the man had already slumped lifeless to the floor at her feet, his eyes bulging glassily. Sophie couldn't tell what was real any what was a memory anymore. She tried to scan the room for any sign of Max, to see if her baby brother was alright, but there was no hint of the other room left. All that was left was shadows. She looked down at the miller at her feet instead, panting.

"You did this, uncle," she heard herself say. "Everything was fine before you came. You did this to all of *us*. You got what you deserved."

The law would not see it that way though, she knew. Her uncle was her guardian and a law-abiding man. Nobody cared what he did behind closed doors as long as he wore the face of respectability. And as long as there were poor old women like Catrin to take the blame for his sins.

She collapsed to her knees, ice pouring through her blood, kissing her trembling skin. Again, she saw that last terrified look on Catrin's face as the villagers hemmed her in and dragged her away, saw the splash as she was tossed, bound, into the middle of the millpond, heard Catrin's last terrified scream echoing again in her ears.

She clenched her hands.

"It's not fair." Tears poured down her numb cheeks. The same people who would hang her for her uncle's death were all gleefully complicit in Catrin's. "No. No, I won't stand for it. I'll make it right. I can. I must."

Wiping her tears away with frozen fingers, she scrambled for her bedding in the corner. Folks didn't usually sleep in the mill itself, but ever since her uncle had moved into the mill house, she had been camping out here. It was better to sleep in the noisy, draughty cold than under the same roof as *him*.

She glanced at his body on the floor. Well. That was one thing at least she would never have to worry about again. Murder was a cardinal sin, of course, and she ought to regret it, but somehow she couldn't bring herself to.

She scrabbled through the mouldering pile of damp blankets she'd taken to sleeping on lately, ousting Catrin's black cat, Smoke, from his slumber. She pulled out the bag of treasure Catrin had entrusted to her. She unwrapped them hastily, staring through the little items: the tools, the journal, the mirror. Her face stared back at her from the mirror's surface, oddly unfamiliar. She had the strangest feeling that her skin was normally more sun-kissed than this porcelain pale face staring back at her, and that her hair should have been shorter and darker, not the long auburn plait frizzing free from its ribbon. The idea sat strangely in her mind, disjointed from the truth before her, but she dismissed it. There was no time left to fret over her exhausted fancies. Smoke swished his tail, glaring at her with suspicion.

The paper rustled as she frantically flicked through to the last pages of the journal. She knew it was in there somewhere. It had been one of their very last conversations, all about the arrival of the witchfinder general. Beth had *known* it was bringing trouble; she had warned Catrin to flee whilst she could, but Catrin had been naïve and stubborn—believing in justice and the law—that innocents would never be blamed for things they hadn't done.

I've helped people with herbs, but I've never hexed anyone, she'd said. *That's what he cares about really. He won't prosecute someone who's never done anything but helped folks.*

Beth blinked away the tears, wishing she could turn back time and *make* Catrin listen.

"You should have hexed him, Catrin," she muttered. "You should have got him before he could get you. That's the only thing that works in this life."

But Catrin, good, patient, kind and gentle, had never seen life like that. She wouldn't have been the Catrin who Beth knew and loved if she had.

Her eyes snagged on the scrawl halfway down the page.

Stay away from hexes, child. They're a wicked, dark magic and they leave a stain everywhere they go.

The words before her swam as her eyes blurred. She could almost hear them in Catrin's melodic tones now. She swallowed hard and skipped ahead, ignoring the warning. She'd stain the whole world if she had to. She'd stain her own soul.

Ah, here. She smiled in relief, her finger running over the words as she read them.

Yew berries hold a dark deadly magic in them. No doubt the witchfinder general will be looking for evidence of whether folks have used them or not. They're dangerous things, child. Used properly, people say that they can trap a spirit or swap it with another.

Her heart stuttered in her chest, hope bubbling within that terrible roiling rage that swirled there.

Swap it with another? Would that not be true justice? Bringing innocent Catrin back in exchange for the people who had hurt her?

She glanced over at her uncle's body and her jaw tightened. Well, she was already a killer now, her soul was already forfeit. And some people, it seemed to her right then, *deserved* to die.

She barely saw the next words; s*uch wicked-dark hexes are full difficult to undo once they have been wrought, for they are tangled up in many strands all together, which must be severed all at once. The site of the hex is important, the strength of feeling it is made with, the talisman it is anchored to, all of these combine to make a powerful working, and all of them must be recombined if you ever changed your mind about it. No, my dear, it is a dark and bitter magic indeed. It is best to leave it all alone, I trow.*

"But I can't, Catrin," she murmured aloud. "Not if there's a chance to save you. Not if there's a single moment of hope that there might be true justice in this forsaken land."

She picked up her skirts and fled through the empty mill to the gardens outside. The moon was high, painting everything navy and silver, except the millpond, which was a startling black. She shuddered away from it and didn't glance into its depths as she scurried, bare-foot, towards the yew bushes which lined the borders of these lands. The rough bark and branches tore at her fingers as she snatched at them with a hasty abandon, but she didn't stop, ripping out berries by the handful, piling them into her apron.

She glanced up at the silent skies above as she worked. It was night still, but she didn't have long. By dawn the village would awake again and all hope of escape would be lost forever. She needed to hurry. She had to resurrect Catrin and get them both out of here long before any witnesses awoke...

The wind blew the door of the mill as she re-entered. It sounded to her frantic imagination like demons knocking to come in, waiting to whisk her away as she damned her soul forever.

"For Catrin," she muttered feverishly as she flung the berries into Catrin's old mortar and pestle and crushed them remorselessly. "Would I not risk even my very soul for her sake?"

Her hands trembled all the same as she coated the knife in the yew berry juice and began muttering beneath her breath, solidifying her intention with the force of her feeling as she squeezed Catrin's old *Maen Magi* stone tightly in her fist, latching it onto the latent magic already inherent in the talisman anchor.

"A life to swap. I need a life to swap for Catrin's..." The words blurred into one another as she gabbled them beneath her breath. She should have swapped her uncle's miserable life for Catrin's, but she had already spent it already. Her eyes fell on Smoke, curled up on the damp blankets once more. His tail flicked through his dreams and guilt squirmed through her stomach—far more guilt than she had felt wrenching that garotte tight around her uncle's leering throat.

"I'm sorry," she whispered, tears prickling in her eyes. "I'm sorry, Smoke, but I can't lose Catrin. I just can't. Forgive me, if you can."

But she squeezed her eyes tight shut as the old vegetable knife sank in.

She could feel the crackle of magic take hold as she squeezed the talisman, Catrin's *Maen Magi* stone, tightly—could feel it fizzing in her fingers, shifting in the air. There was an odd weight to it, a sheeny, greasy, slippery heft that slipped through the clean air of the house, tainting it. But Beth couldn't worry about that now.

I just need Catrin back. Bring me Catrin back.

She tried to sense the fading lifeforce and pull it

forwards out of the air, binding it with poor Smoke's dwindling aura, trading them by the power of the yew berries. Something shifted.

It's working!

Beside her, her uncle's foot twitched.

She yelped, staring at it in horror.

He's still alive? I must just have knocked him unconscious, after all. I should—

But far too late, the realisation grew in her. She glanced between the talisman clutched in her hand and his body as it began to twitch and gasp, empty eyed and hollow, his eyelids fluttering over his cloudy vision.

"No," she gasped. "No, it's the wrong spirit! I've brought the wrong life back!"

"Beth," he croaked, his voice creakier than gallow-wood, barely more than a hoarse exhalation.

"No!" It was just too cruel, to have returned her tormentor and not her friend. She snatched at the yew laden knife and drove it deep into her uncle's chest, stilling him once more. His breath slipped away again, but that strange weight in the air did not.

Beth.

Her own name echoed around her head in that

last bitter breath, her uncle's tones repeating it again and again.

"It's just a memory. Just a nightmare."

But she wasn't sure she believed it.

Gingerly, she pulled the knife from his chest. She had to get rid of the evidence. She couldn't leave him here now. Bury him. That was the thing to do. Be free of him once and for all.

No. I'll drown him. That would be justice.

Jutting her chin out, she fumbled her arms under the corpse's heavy shoulders, hauled the body up under its arms and dragged it out of the mill. A smear of blood and dirt swept like a snail's sticky trail behind them both. The splash as she cast it into the water and watched it sink slowly out of sight was immense.

She glanced at the skies. Still dark. She had time to try again.

Beth. Beth. What have you done? Her uncle's voice whispered in her ears as the night breeze swept around her. She squeezed her eyes tightly shut, blinking away the tears swelling there.

"The hex works," she muttered to herself. "I know it works, at least. I just need another life to swap for Catrin's, make sure I get the right soul back this time..."

She cast around desperately for a fox or a badger, an owl—anything! *Anyone*. But the night was mockingly empty.

Her gaze drifted through the woods to the distant glow of the golden windows in the mill house beyond.

The witchfinder general is still there.

She froze as the idea slowly began to form. Her uncle had been boasting to all and sundry that the witchfinder general, Matthew , had deigned to stay with him. And it was because Uncle Llewelyn had lavished him with such fine foods and wines that the witchfinder had decided to find Catrin guilty to repay the favour, she was all but sure.

It would be risky, and yet, is there not an ironic sense of justice in it too?

Slowly, she reached for her knife once more.

For Catrin's sake, and for all the other innocents has murdered too. It will stop him hurting anyone else. It is more justice than the law would ever give me.

She believed that, and she would go on believing it, even if it forfeited her very soul.

"Help me, oh, please, help," she wept theatrically,

stumbling through the front door of the mill house not five minutes later.

Matthew was sat by the large hearth, his booted feet up on the fender, his pipe stuck in his mouth. He eyed her with a mixture of curl-lipped repulsion and a strange, unwilling desire—as if the fact that he could not deny her beauty disgusted him.

"What is it?" he snapped.

She clutched at his hands, summoning yet more tears to her eyes. "Magic, sir," she said on a trembling breath. "More wicked witchcraft, out by the mill where you drowned Goody Waterhouse. I think it's got my uncle. Please, come and help me."

Matthew was up to his feet at once, drawing out his flintlock pistol. Beth eyed it unhappily. Those newfangled weapons were notoriously unreliable, of course, but that was small comfort. They didn't need to be reliable. The mere sight of them was enough to keep most people in line.

A vicious thing, only made for killing, and yet he happily wields it whilst he blames others for the same sins.

"Well, girl, where is it then? Lead on," he snapped, and she bobbed into a small, trembling curtsey, tugging him out into the night.

THE WATER MILL

The path between the mill house and the mill itself was always hard to traverse, even by daylight. By the veiled light of the moon now, it was almost impossible. The ground sloped downwards into the dell, matted with thorny bushes and hedges. In the dim glow of starlight, Beth snatched a handful of berries from the yew bush on the way past. She surreptitiously smeared them along the blade of her knife as she led him onwards to his doom, trying to summon up the right intentions for the hex. The witchfinder general didn't seem to notice.

"Well?" he snapped. "What's the problem then? Where's this uncle of yours. I'd better speak to him in person. I'll get more commonsense out of that man than from a silly feather-brained girl."

"He went into the millpond, sir." She forced her voice to come out breathless and trembling, making her eyes as wide and frightened as she could. "He said something was drawing him into it, something he could not resist or fight. I think he might have gone under the waters, sir. I think he might be drowning!"

The witchfinder general's sharp, angular face tightened in the moonlight. He cocked his pistol and, instinctively, Beth flinched away. It was not many men who could afford such a weapon—but then, witchfinder generals were always wealthy, powerful men, she had heard. They didn't content themselves with the power they already had. They were always, always hungry for more.

And he'll never stop. Not unless I can make him.

Resolve swelled through her. This was a wicked thing she was doing, and she knew it well. But she did not believe it was *more* wicked than the damage he had wrought. And if he was not going to stop, then neither could she.

She shifted the blade in her hand, taking a firmer grip on it.

The witchfinder general stepped towards the pond, aiming the pistol to its surface. The waters were so perfectly still that they seemed almost glass-like, putting Beth in mind of Catrin's scrying mirror. Not a single shadow moved on them.

The witchfinder general growled and rounded on her once more, discarding his gun. She couldn't help but notice that relief was echoing there with the anger in his eyes though.

"There's nothing there, girl," he snapped. "I suppose you think that's funny, do you? Play a jape on the witchfinder general to amuse yourself. Lure him away to make a fool of him. I'll show you better." His eyes gleamed wickedly as he put a hand around her throat. "I was wrong, it seems," he whispered, pulling her up close to his body and staring down at her. His breath misted in the night between them, his eyes, fervent and furious, gleaming darkly. "I thought you could still be saved if I cut out the source of your corruption, but the apprentice has become the master, it seems. You have dabbled too far in witchcraft, like your iniquitous mistress, and must also be dealt with for the greater good. You are beyond salvation now."

A small smile spread across Beth's face then. "Perhaps," she whispered. "But so are you."

And she stabbed him, hard and fast. He gasped, his eyes widening, inches from her own as she felt the hot spurt of his blood oozing over them both. He staggered backwards, splashing into the millpond, staring down at his stomach, placing trembling fingers over the hole there, spilling entrails and flesh.

He fell to his knees, gaping at her in a final mixture of surprise, horror and anger and then fell backwards with a splash.

For a moment, Beth just stood there on the edge

of the water, trembling, coated in his blood. The moonlight shone down at them all, glinting on the corpse bobbing on the surface of the dark pond, blood seeping from his body, almost painting the dark waters black.

"Don't just stand there," she chided herself through chattering teeth. "Quickly, before it is too late."

She summoned all her intentions, clinging onto the mix of crushed yew berries and sacrificial blood.

Suddenly, her eyes shot open. "The talisman! I forgot to get a talisman!"

It was too late now. The hex was already forming and taking hold. She could feel it swirling around her. She'd just have to trust it was strong enough to latch onto a nearby magical object on its own.

She closed her eyes again and fumbled through the strands of auras rising from the millpond. This time, she didn't just snatch at the closest one, she felt for the one that seemed most like Catrin. Kind. Patient. Gentle. The only aura here without a hint of malice or greed.

She tangled it around her fingers like a skein of wool and *tugged*.

The world shifted. She could feel it answering

her call. This was power! This was *life.* Her eyes flew open and she half expected to see Catrin there, rising from the middle of the pond with her old familiar smile on her face, wringing out her sopping skirts. The pond was empty still.

"No. Come *on,* Catrin. Come back to me. Don't leave me alone here like this."

Her gaze scoured the rippling surface of the waters—and then her heart leapt to her throat. There! There in the water! A face, rising to the surface! Pale and terrified but wonderfully familiar. Beth tried to wade into the waters to help her out, but Catrin thrust a hand towards her, her mouth framing a frantic, silent, *no!*

Beth couldn't move.

"Catrin! Catrin, come out! Let me help you! We need to flee!"

But Catrin was just as trapped as Beth was, it seemed. She could not break the surface of the water either.

"No," Beth wept, struggling desperately, trying to reach her friend, so close yet so hopelessly far away.

Catrin was not at peace, as all good souls should be, but she was not able to fully return either. She was trapped between the two states, and it was all Beth's fault.

Beth flinched suddenly. At first, she thought it was just a trick of the moonlight, but now she could see it clearly. Two dark shadows were manifesting there behind Catrin, vicious, cruel, consumed by their own violence and rage.

Matthew and my Uncle Llewelyn.

The spirit of the witchfinder general moved forwards. She could feel his ill intentions locking onto her, seeking her destruction even from beyond the grave. She stumbled backwards, but he could not break the surface of the waters either, it seemed. He roared, wordlessly, and the still surface of the pond began to churn, ripple and rise towards her. She stumbled another step backwards. He was going to flood the mill—he was going to drag her under by force.

Everything within her was telling her to flee, but she couldn't leave Catrin like this, surrounded by the men who had killed her, trapped in the pool that had claimed her life.

beckoned. Beth's limbs lurched forwards instinctively. She tried to fight it. She screamed and clenched every muscle, trying to stop the inexorable stumble towards the grave. Her feet splashed into the edges of the water and ice flooded her toes. She could feel waves of malignant glee flooding the night.

They're going to drown me. We're all going to end together here tonight.

beckoned again, his aura spreading through the waters as he strained all his strength towards her, until almost the whole millpond was a dark and eerie black.

She took another step forwards. Icy fingers clasped around her ankle, tried to pull her down. She wobbled.

No! Beth!

She heard Catrin screaming. There was a great thrust of power and she was shoved backwards, out of the edge of the water, scrabbling through the churned earth, released from 's power.

She heard a great roar echoing distantly through the night, the waters churning and bubbling before her in fury. Beth backed away, trembling, her hands, still stained with yew berries and blood, fleeing to her lips.

"What have I done?" she whispered. "Oh, Catrin, I only wanted to help. I only wanted you *back*. What have I *done?*"

Catrin's eyes met hers across the rippling

waters, terrified and hollow, but glinting with the same compassion they always had.

"Go," Catrin mouthed silently. "Flee!"

And Beth obeyed. She ran into the mill, snatching up Catrin's treasures and the body of the rigid Smoke, which she lovingly swaddled, the last gift she could give him now. The mirror had shattered, a spider's web of cracks splintering the middle of it, as if something heavy had collided with its centre. Her heart wanted to weep as she picked it up. Catrin had been so grateful for the gift. She had showed Beth how to use it to clear her mind and summon glimpses of the future—but neither of them had ever spotted this sore fate within it. Catrin had said that she had seen someone in it, sometimes. A woman, warm and loving, staring back at her—a friend she could not reach but would have trusted with her life.

And where was your friend now, Catrin? She abandoned you, just as I must. Oh, Catrin, oh, my friend. You deserved so much better.

But she did not have time to linger, even amongst such bitter regrets. Wiping her tears away hastily, she shoved all these treasures behind the loose panel in the back room of the mill, negotiating the panel back into place with difficulty with her numb, frozen fingers. She sealed it shut with a smear of blood and a fervent oath, so that nothing but her own blood could open it again. They would be safe now, as they would need to be. She would need these very items to break Catrin's curse and free her spirit once more, she was sure.

"I'll be back," she vowed hoarsely, backing away from the wall. "As soon as I find a way to undo what I have done to you, Catrin, I will make it right again. I swear it."

And then, tears still streaming from her eyes, she stumbled away out into the night alone—always, always alone. Invisible hands grabbed at her roughly. She tried to bat them away but could not. They tugged at her, shook her, arrested her as she tried to flee.

Sophie, frantic, disembodied voices shrieked. *You have to wake up! Sophie! Come back to us!*

"Sophie?" Beth said faintly. "Who's—"

But then she opened her eyes.

Her mum was standing a few inches away, her hands were claws on Sophie's shoulders as they stood in the dying afternoon light on the front driveway. A horde of the local villagers stood behind her watching, horror-struck. Gravel crunched underfoot where just seconds ago there had been soft, churned earth, and the starless night had been blinked back into a golden glow. Her muddy woollen skirts were once again strategically ripped jeans, and her hands were clean and bloodless once more.

But the weight of Beth's anger, fear and grief still sat stone-like in her stomach—and the memory of what she had done still stained her mind.

"Max?" Sophie gasped, clutching at her mum. "Is he...?" She could bring herself to say *dead*, not when it might well have been her own hands which throttled him.

Her mother let out a burble of hysterical laughter, hauling her into a fierce hug. "Alive," she assured her, tears still cascading down her face, and Sophie sank to her knees in great sobbing convulsions of relief. "You both are my darling. He was unconscious when we found him and he says he can't remember what happened, but he's alright. There's no lasting damage done, we think."

Sophie clung all the tighter to her mother, as if she could anchor herself back to reality by clinging onto that old and paint-flecked jumper. "It was Beth," she said huskily. "She was the one who trapped them all in the millpond. She didn't mean to, but she did it, and then she fled."

She glanced over at the malevolently rippling

waters beside her. Four hundred years or more Catrin had been trapped in there with the men who had murdered her. Beth was right. She did deserve better.

She stumbled to her feet. Her legs felt hollow and wobbly, but she forced them to take her weight. "I think I know now how we can undo it," she said.

CHAPTER 9
THE RITUAL OF RELEASE

Abbie paused for a moment on the upper landing, taking a breath. The moonlight was streaming through the window, but the house wasn't still. Even here, in this stolen moment of peace, soft noises drifted through the house.

She glanced back towards Max's bedroom. He hadn't made any fuss about going to bed tonight, which was most unlike him, and he asked her to leave the landing light on. He hadn't slept with a night light since he was five years old. But though he was clearly scared, his eyes were clear, and his breathing was regular, and he hadn't fallen into any unexplained fits of rage. She thought the moment had passed safely by, and that he was OK.

Or, at least, he will be, just as soon as this whole mess is sorted out once and for all.

She ran her hands through her hair with a huff, trying to summon up the last dwindling dregs of her strength now. Hushed voices drifted up from the studio downstairs as the people from the village gathered to help. Something twisted in Abbie's stomach. It didn't really seem fair that she and John could rely on the kindness of strangers to help them, when Catrin and Beth had been so cruelly used and abandoned.

Would I have tried to help if I had been alive there at the time? Or would I have turned a blind eye, like everyone else?

She didn't know. But she was doing what she could now. She'd just have to hope it was enough... She took one last deep breath and went down to join the others below.

They were all gathered around the art table in the studio, cradling mismatched mugs of tea and passing around a plate of chocolate hobnobs, avoiding each other's eyes. Sophie, sitting next to John, was the youngest here by decades, save for Dafydd and Rhiannon, Cerys' kids. Dafydd, who could only have been a year or two older than Sophie, was staring at Soph, a look of punch-drunk wonder on his face. But that was a problem for another day, Abbie decided.

She sat beside her daughter and took her hand.

"Alright," she said into the expectantly waiting silence. "Max is down now. Soph, why don't you go ahead and fill us in?"

Sophie squeezed her fingers and then got to her feet. Although she pinked a little at the weight of all those gazes staring at her, she explained precisely and clearly what she had seen that afternoon. She held up the journal and flipped to the last pages, running her hands tenderly over the fading cursive scrawl there.

"I saw her reading from here," she said, looking around at the gathered adults. "The hex has trapped the spirits together. We need to break all the threads that bind them together to release them and let them go free once more." She ticked them off on her fingers. "The place, which is the millpond. The feeling which conjured it, which was the anger and fear of the community. And the talisman which binds them. The first talisman she tried was the witchstone, the *Maen Magi,* she called it, but I'm not sure if one talisman could be reused twice. And if it can't, then she must have used a second talisman for the second spell, and I don't know what that could be. She didn't remember to fetch one in time, so she just had to hope it would attach itself to the closest magical object available. I wondered whether it might have been the millpond itself, but according to the journal, talismans are immutable. The millpond changes far too often to make that true. I suppose it could be the journal itself. It's definitely going to be an object with a lot of innate magic in it, that's for sure."

Innate magic?

Abbie startled as a thought occurred to her.

"If it's highly magical, odd things will happen around it. What have you noticed like that?" Cerys piped up from the other side of the table.

"Well, the journal keeps reappearing of its own free will, and I can read it, though I shouldn't be able to—" Sophie began, but a shiver had run over Abbie's skin.

"No," she whispered, certainty flooding her. "It's not the journal. It's the scrying mirror. I've been seeing glimpses of Catrin's past through it. Part of Catrin is trapped in it. It's the second talisman, I'm certain of it."

She glanced at John, and he nodded back at her. "So," he said. "We've got the millpond, the help of the village and the talisman. Is there anything else we need before we can get started undoing this hex?"

"We need to be outside. We cannot do it here," Abbie said. "We need to end this where it first began. If you are ready, willing and able to help us end this, everyone, then we must go to the millpond now."

But John stopped them as they rose to go. "Wait. You need to be prepared," he said softly, his eyes haunted and agonised. "The darkness in that water will not give in without a fight. It will make you feel things—*do* things—you never thought possible. Anger beyond anything you've ever felt before will overtake you." He looked around at the men as he said this, Mr Edwards, little Dai Bach—a square, balding, cheery man, whose beer belly was almost as big as his grin—and Dafydd, Cerys' son. Then he glanced up at the ceiling, as if he could see Max, sleeping above them. "It even infected Max, my son, and he's just a boy. You *must* be on your guard against it. You must hold on."

Abbie squeezed his hand, longing to tell him that it wasn't his fault, but not knowing how to in front of all these witnesses. He squeezed her hand back tightly, so perhaps he understood.

"There is fear too," she murmured. "Panic. Pain.

But it is just a memory. It feels real, heaven knows, but it is imposed upon you from the outside, it does not come from within. It can be fought."

"Well, that's why we're here. To fight!" Cerys said fiercely. Her children exchanged looks of loving exasperation and Abbie smiled slightly. "This has gone on long enough."

They got to their feet without another word, filing out as silently as monks in a monastery. The moonlight rose above the tree line, shadows dancing and splitting across the fragmented lights. The night was cold. Abbie concentrated on the steady beating of her pulse, and the misty wraiths of her breath to centre herself against the burgeoning panic which threatened to claim her.

*I am more powerful than a nightmare. I am not going to run. **They** should be afraid of **me.***

The wind whistled as they took their places, spreading out around the murky depths of the millpond. The mist rose, obscuring them, so that Abbie could barely see those who had taken their places on the far side now.

I must trust that they will hold their nerve. We all depend on each other now, as a true community should.

She glanced over at John, who had taken his place beside her. His jaw was taut, and his eyes were troubled, but he shot her a quick smile and a reassuring nod. Sophie stood on the other side, the fractured scrying mirror clasped tightly in one hand, the journal in the other. She wasn't looking at Abbie. Her gaze was fixed on the waters before them.

Abbie took a deep breath and held up the glass she'd brought to fetch out the millpond water for the ritual.

"Give it here," John said tersely. "I'll fetch the water."

But Abbie stopped him, shaking her head. "This is my job. I owe it to Catrin to finish this myself."

His brow creased. "It's dangerous, Abs. And you don't owe her anything. You weren't the one who killed her!"

But she did owe it to Catrin. She knew it in a way she couldn't have explained to him, deep down in her bones. And what was more, she owed it to herself too.

She stepped forwards. The mist thickened, the cold air of the night scratching at her skin, but she would not be frightened away now. She knelt at the edge of the water. It rippled faster than ever, looking oily black and almost greasy in the darkness. Frantic screams echoed through the hastily rising mists enveloping them all, but they were just memories,

THE WATER MILL

she told herself. Old injustices reverberating through these lands. They could not harm her now.

The clunk of the waterwheel began once more. Every sonorous clank seemed to wrap itself around her like ghostly chains, binding her inescapably in this moment. She swallowed dryly. A now familiar face began slowly to appear in the shadows of the waterweeds and algae. Dark, desperate eyes locked onto hers. Panic—raw and wild—flooded her, everything within her screaming at her to flee, every muscle bunched and taut.

It's just Catrin. She's trying to frighten me away to protect me from the witchfinder general. I will not give into it. I will not be ousted now.

But Abbie's hands quavered all the same, as she dipped them below the surface of the millpond to scoop some water out.

Icy fingers clasped around her wrist from beneath the water, tugging her hand deeper beneath the rippling waves. Abbie screamed. She tried to scrabble backwards, but that cruel grasp was immovable. It was pulling her deeper into the waters, until she was up to her elbow in it now, then further, almost up to her shoulder. It was going to pull her in entirely.

A hacking, choking laugh, sinister and deep,

swept through the night around her as ice washed up her arm—across her chest—around her whole body—but she had no idea whether anyone else could hear it, or if they were inside her mind now—trapped within her, lodged there inescapably.

"Abbie!"

Far warmer hands seized her other wrist. She looked up. John was beside her, clinging onto her tightly, throwing his whole weight back to the gravel beyond to stop her sliding any further in. She was torn between the two, until she thought her shoulders might dislocate, or she might split down the middle entirely.

"I've got you now, it's alright," Mr Edwards called, hurrying up to help. He was quickly outpaced by Rhiannon and Dafydd, then by Dai Bach, by Cerys and Mari—by almost everyone, in fact. They had all abandoned their positions around the pool to cling onto her, the villagers coming together to save one innocent woman from drowning needlessly.

The perfect mirror to the original crime.

Only Sophie remained in position. She was still standing there, shut-eyed in the moonlight, the journal in one hand, the scrying mirror in the other, muttering beneath her breath.

The claws around Abbie's wrist dug in deeper,

biting through her skin, and she slipped a little deeper into the waters despite the clutch of warm, desperate hands snatching her back. She tried to pull the glass out of the water, but she wasn't strong enough.

The millpond began to rise, thrashing, bubbling, roiling madly. It looked as though it was boiling, lit from below by the fires of hell, but it was icy cold, leeching all the warmth from her skin until her hand was numb. She tried again to pull herself away, even releasing the glass to try to yank her fingers loose. It didn't work. She was trapped, and still the waters rose. She leaned back as far as she could, tilting her head up to the moonlight.

"Cerys, get your kids away from here," she whispered, tears piling in her eyes. "All of you, get away. They're going to drown us all. Save yourselves whilst you can."

"We're not going anywhere," Dafydd said fiercely, and a chorus of agreement rose at his words which warmed Abbie through even here, in the midst of this panic.

The waterwheel rattled around faster than ever. The doors of the mill house began to slam as though a strong wind was blowing them, though there wasn't even a hint of a breeze here now. Ghostly shutters began rattling in the windows too, and the disembodied yowl and spit of a cat split the air.

Sophie was chanting something now, but Abbie couldn't understand it. Her face seemed paler than ever, and her hair, usually the same chestnut brown as Abbie's own, seemed almost auburn in the moonlight, as though it were aflame.

The waters were churning higher than ever, up to Abbie's neck as she knelt on the floor. It was spilling over the knees of the surrounding villagers as they still clung bravely to her, trying to stop her from slipping any further in.

"I can't get the water to Sophie for the ritual," Abbie whispered to John as he grunted and swore beside her. Tears streamed down her face. What if they all died here like this? What if Sophie died too? Abbie should never have involved her; she should have insisted that Sophie stayed away. And Max, upstairs asleep! What if he woke in the morning to find his whole family had drowned in the night? What would become of her baby?

"Sophie!" John screamed suddenly.

Abbie looked over and froze, horror threading through her. Sophie was walking straight towards the rising waters.

"Go to her, John," Abbie pleaded.

John glanced down at her, anguished indecision stark on his face.

Abbie took a deep, wavering breath and tried to project her calmest self. "You can't save us both," she whispered, burying her head in his neck as he clung to her. "Choose our daughter. I want you to. She deserves to live. Please, John, for me. Please, before it is too late."

He hesitated for a fraction of a second more, tears caught in his eyes, then he gave her a last fierce, frenzied kiss, and a muttered *I love you, Abs* before he released her, sprinting towards the slowly stumbling Sophie.

Abbie slipped a little further into the rising waters. She took a deep breath, her eyes fixed on John as he grabbed Sophie around the waist—

—and then Abbie went under the rising tide of icy waters completely.

~

Anger was pounding through John now, but he couldn't tell which was the spirits' wrath and which was his own. That these monsters were not content enough to kill innocents in their own lifetime, that they should still be murdering guiltless women all these years later, and that now they had sought his own family, who had done nothing wrong save stumble into the wrong place at the wrong time? It was too much to bear.

He roared, his rage spurring him onwards, leaping over the uneven gravel and snatching Sophie around the waist just as she was about to enter the waters. She thrashed in his arms.

He glanced over his shoulder, still trying to haul her away. He couldn't see Abs at all.

"Don't worry about Mum, Catrin's with her," Sophie said. "She'll be alright. Leave the others to me."

And she sounded so calmly confident, so strangely assured amid all this panic and chaos, that for a split second, John released his grip.

And a second was all it took. Sophie plunged forwards, diving fearlessly beneath the waves themselves, still clutching onto the journal and the mirror. John let out a wild oath. He followed her in.

The icy kiss of the water consumed him, tensing every muscle in his body at once. It was so dark, so murky. He couldn't tell which way was up anymore as it swirled around him in muddled hazes. He tried to hold his breath as the shadows swirled around him, but there were so many faces here, all around him, leading him down, deeper, inevitably.

Sophie, where are you?

He would have loved to scream her name, but the acrid taste of bitter waters was already seeping down his throat through his tightly pressed lips.

A yowl resounded, far clearer than it had ever sounded before. There, in the murky gloom, a shadow of a cat, larger than a panther, was arched and hissing at Sophie who was floating there serenely, her hair haloing around her in slow, dreamy waves.

No, he realised as he swam towards it hurriedly, it wasn't hissing at Sophie. It was standing before her, hissing and spitting at the other, dark shadows drifting forwards malevolently. It was trying to keep them at bay.

Sophie, he screamed within his mind once more, wishing she could hear him. She didn't turn. She didn't seem the least bit perturbed at all, in fact, as he thrashed his way forwards for her.

His lungs were screaming at him, but he didn't kick for the surface. He wouldn't. Not without Sophie. Her eyes were shut, but her expression was serene. She still held on tightly to the journal and the mirror.

The shadow before them solidified in a man's face, sharp, angular and furious. He cast the cat aside with a vicious wave, stretching out for Sophie.

You will never have my daughter.

John surged past Sophie, and spread himself out as wide as he could, trying to use his own body to block the stranger from reaching Sophie. The stranger's dark eyes met John's. The shadow smiled and swooped. It moved *into* John, filling him entirely.

John let out an *oh* of surprise, the breath he had been straining to keep fleeing from his lips in a string of bubbles. The stale water rushed into his lungs, but it didn't drown him. It couldn't anymore. He was part of the water itself, he was the malevolence of the millpond, he was the shadow in the water, it could not harm him now.

Good, a voice purred in his head. *Yes. There is much work still to be done. And it will be accomplished more easily with a body to do it in. I have waited a long time to be about my business. Wickedness must be eradicated. Order must be restored. We must kill them all. Purge the land. Drown the witch.*

He turned towards the wicked enchantress floating there behind him, seducing good men into the ways of sinners and the unrighteous. There was a magical glow around her now. He could see it consuming her. Her eyes turned to his and he recognised them, dark and vengeful, from that night. The body might be different, but the soul was the same. She was still the same evil slattern who had lured him down here, pretending to be helpless and innocent. The same harlot who had trapped him here for spite's sake for hundreds of years. He smiled and stretched out a hand for her, ready to close it around her throat and drag her down here to damnation with him where they would have an eternity of torment and turmoil awaiting them—

—and John closed his fingers into a fist.

No. Not my daughter. Not this time. It ends with us.

Sophie—Beth—smiled. The last of the bubbles streamed from her mouth, her eyes rolled back into her head as she went limp and a roll of strange, vicious triumph surged through John, fighting with the panic and fear overwhelming him.

No! Not Sophie!

Yes, death to all witches!

But then Sophie's eyes shot open once more. She thrust a hand out towards him and a great wave rushed across the pond, sending him spiralling through the waters, dizzy and disorientated.

A distant roar echoed through his mind, but it was cut short into echoing silence.

John blinked.

Abruptly, his throat burned, his vision swam and the desperate clawing need for air was upon him once more. With the last burst of his strength, he snatched his daughter around the waist and kicked for the surface. They broke into the freezing night air together, snatching down glorious lungfuls of oxygen as he dragged her to the shore.

"Is it done?" he croaked hoarsely, his throat still burning. He turned to the water, searching desperately for any sign of dark magic. The waters were no longer rippling, no shadows lurked in their depths—it even seemed like a lighter shade of murky brown now, rather than its previous glimmering onyx. Whatever spirits had been lingering there were gone, it seemed. The floodwaters had even subsided, and as he stared around at the waters' edge, he saw Abbie had been released from the millpond's grip too. She had been hauled to the gravel driveway and Dai was performing CPR on her.

His heart stuttered, all relief fleeing from him at once.

No. Not my Abbie. She can't be dead.

He stared, frozen in horror at the still, lifeless body of his wife. Everything within him was screaming at him to run to her, to shake her awake, to bring her back to herself—to do something, anything, to make this not be happening. His useless limbs refused to move.

Sophie was still eerily calm. She hardly seemed perturbed at all, in fact.

She walked slowly over to her mother, past the weeping Mari and Cerys, who was trying to phone for an ambulance, and she pushed Dai away. She closed her eyes and, though John couldn't be sure, he thought she might have muttered something.

Instantly, Abbie spluttered up to one elbow, spewing out stale water and bile.

All the air rushed into John's lungs at once and he dived towards her, gathering her into his arms, weeping.

How? How is this possible?

But he wouldn't question it now. Perhaps it was just one last gift from Beth. He looked over at Sophie. She nodded.

"What's that?" he whispered urgently, staring at the strange, empty wooden frame in her hand as he clutched Abbie to him with one hand and Sophie to him with the other. "Where did you get it from? It's not—" He couldn't finish that sentence, couldn't put into words the growing doubt flooding him that this whole mad nightmare wasn't truly over yet.

"It's only the frame of the scrying mirror," she replied, still in that uncannily serene way.

He gasped. "The glass! It's gone!"

"Yes," she said. "It splintered into a thousand fragments, and each of them are lying at rest in the bottom of the millpond."

He clutched Abbie and Sophie to his sodden chest even tighter, if such a thing was possible. "And the witchfinder general? Catrin? Are they at rest too?"

And Sophie's smile was wide, bright and beautifully genuine as she whispered just two small words in the moonlight.

"They're gone."

CHAPTER 10
THE QUIET MILL

The aftermath of such a chaotic battle was oddly anticlimactic, Abbie thought. She stared around at their new friends, each clutching each other.

Catrin was gone at last. Abbie had known it even before Sophie had confirmed it. After all, Catrin had been there with Abbie in the murky darkness of the millpond waters, right at the end.

Abbie shuddered. She'd remember that moment as long as she lived, she was sure. The electric moment of panic as she sucked in one last breath and slipped beneath the waters. The swirling shadows had tried to claim her, but Catrin had held them at bay—saving Abbie's soul, even if she could no longer save her body. Even when it looked like all hope was gone, Catrin had not relented. She truly was the bravest woman Abbie had ever met. And, when Sophie and John had crashed into the centre of the pond too, distracting Matthew away from Abbie once more, Catrin had stayed there with her.

Go, Abbie had willed her with her last, straining breath as the fizzing greyness ate at the corners of her vision and the muted rumble of waters clogged her ears, making her dizzy and light-headed. *Save Sophie. Save my daughter.*

But Catrin hadn't left. She had *smiled.* And though Abbie couldn't have said why, a great feeling of peace and confidence had swept over her as the darkness rushed into claim her. And she hadn't remembered anything else until she found herself looking up at Sophie on the muddy shore of the millpond again. She would probably never really know what Catrin had done in that moment, but it didn't really matter. Catrin had saved her—saved Sophie—saved them all, just as she had once saved Beth. And she was at peace at last, of that, Abbie was certain.

She pushed her damp hair out of her face, shivering with cold, and looked around. The mill water was eerily quiet now, calm and still, as if it had never been anything else. She felt, perhaps, that they ought to say something, some speech, maybe, or some commemorative moment, but nothing came to mind, so she just turned to the others. They were watching her with a wary silence, as if not sure who she was anymore.

"Tea?" she asked.

They stared at her, and then Cerys let out a great burble of hysterical laughter. Soon, everyone joined in. They were all laughing, clasping onto each other to hold upright, wheezing through their tears as they howled.

The front door opened, and Max stood there, framed in the threshold in his pyjamas. "What's going on?" he asked, rubbing his eyes. "What's so funny?"

And right at that moment, Abbie thought they couldn't have asked for a better moment. They were alive. They were together. They were laughing.

She turned to the waters, though they were wonderfully empty now. "Thank you, Catrin," she whispered.

And she knew it was just her imagination, but she couldn't help but think that the glitter of the moonlight on the surface was Catrin's way of saying goodbye.

...

Their first Christmas in the mill was certainly a memorable one, Abbie thought. John had been keen to sell up and move on again, not quite trusting that the discontent around the mill was gone now, but Abbie had been resolute. They had survived hellfire and brimstone to be here, they weren't going to walk away from John's dreams now. Besides, the kids were settled in the schools, and the estate agents still didn't think another sale was likely, and, after all, there hadn't been so much as a nightmare between them since that night. True, they were all left a little shaken, given to flinching if the door banged too loudly or if the floorboard creaks could be mistaken for the waterwheel, but they were here, they were alive, and she didn't intend to be chased away by the anger of the past now. They were going to wipe away the horrors of the past with new, happier memories in this, their home. And they were going to start today.

She snuggled up on the sofa, cradling her cup of hot chocolate as Max fetched the presents out from under the tree and handed them around.

Sophie ripped the wrapping paper off her gift first. Her face lit up. "Brilliant, Mum, thanks! It's just what I wanted!"

She held the book up so everyone could see the title. *An introduction to practical witchcraft in the 21st century.*

Beside her on the sofa, John grimaced, but he bit his tongue. Abbie squeezed his hand. He was still very ambivalent about magic, she knew, and less than happy that Sophie was still interested in it. She'd even asked Cerys to give her a few lessons after school—and wasn't young Dafydd rather pleased that Sophie had started popping over so often?

But magic wasn't wrong in itself, surely even John had to see that? Yes, Beth's desperate hex that night had done untold damage for hundreds of years, that could not be denied. But magic had also been used to save them all that night. It wasn't intrinsically bad. Like so much in life, it just depended on how you used it.

"I suppose I should just be grateful you're happy to get a book as a gift," John teased, and Sophie rolled her eyes.

"Mums got a book too, I think. Unless a tea-towel has been very cunningly wrapped," Sophie said, chuckling the wrapped parcel at Abbie.

She unwrapped it and, indeed, found a book

waiting for her within, a field guide to herbs, berries and fungi from her husband.

"Thanks, sweetheart," she murmured, pressing a kiss to John's cheek. She didn't know why she was so interested in it all really, she wasn't intending to follow Sophie down the road of practical magics, after all, but she couldn't walk away from it either. She couldn't help feeling that if she could just understand a little bit more about the herbs Catrin had used, she might understand the whole mess a little better. How the villagers could have been so afraid of a woman who only wanted to help them— how Catrin knew where the line between herb-craft and witchcraft lay—and how Beth could have crossed that line so willingly. The disturbances here might have been put to bed, but there were so many mysteries that still remained, so many unanswered questions. And, though she was beginning to admit to herself that they might never be fully answered, Abbie wasn't going to walk away without trying to understand it a little better, at least. Catrin wouldn't have done, after all. She had never fled from anything.

Besides, it might be nice to grow some heritage herbs in the grounds, just as long as they're not yew berries.

She'd had John rip out all the yew bushes weeks

ago, burning them in a large bonfire in the garden. It was probably just superstition, of course, but Abbie wasn't going to take any chances now. They'd had enough of ghosts and death rites for a while.

"Open your one, love," she said, pointing at the thin package still lingering beneath the tree. Max tossed it over.

"Ooh, it's hard but thin... Is it... a place mat?" he said, shaking it theatrically.

"Just open it already, you'll never guess." She laughed.

John obeyed, ripping the paper off in one fell swoop. He gasped slightly as he looked down at the thin metal sign she'd had engraved for him. "Oh, love. It's beautiful," he said, stroking his fingers softly over the cursive letters.

"What is it?" Max asked from the floor.

John held it up to show him. "It's a sign for our new gallery. We've just submitted the planning permission to build it up on the front drive." He turned to her, happiness beaming from every pore of his face. "It's really happening at last. You're sure you don't mind?"

"Don't mind? Of course not! It's your dream, John, and I love you. I want to make it a reality."

He kissed her, making their children groan.

"Gobaith Gallery," Sophie read. "That's a weird name."

"It means hope in Welsh," Max piped up from the beneath the tree, still scrabbling to fetch out the next presents. "Hope Gallery."

"It just seemed fitting," John said, and Abbie beamed at him.

"Come on. There's still more to unwrap. It's your turn now, Max," she said, squeezing John's hand tightly and snuggling into his side.

Max's face lit up as he unwrapped the gift. He held it up so they could all see it, a genealogy workbook and organiser.

Sophie rolled her eyes. "You're such a geek, Max," she said. "Only you would be excited by that. You do know it's an old man hobby, don't you? Mr Edwards does it. Ten-year-olds are supposed to be interested in like, football and video games and stuff."

"Oh, leave him be," Abbie said indulgently, smiling over at them both. "If it makes him happy, what's the matter?"

"I might even be able to get back as far as the Domesday book now, if I'm lucky," Max said, his eyes gleaming. "I've already got back to the tail end of the seventeenth century, up to Mr Matthew and

Beth Hodges."

Sophie, Abbie and John all startled, staring at each other.

It couldn't be... it would be too much of a coincidence, surely?

"Oh?" Abbie said casually. "Who were they then?"

"Well, Matthew worked in a lawyer's office when he was married, according to the licence. He lived in London. I can't find out much about Beth so far. She'd only just arrived in London when she married him, and she said she had no other living relatives according to the census."

Could she really be our ancestor? Perhaps that was why we were called here. Perhaps that was why we found all her old things, and why she revealed her hiding place? Perhaps that was how Sophie was able to read her journal and perform her spells? Maybe we were the only way that she could make things right at last...

It would be nice to think so, anyway, she thought.

"And was she happy?" she asked quietly.

Max gave her an exasperated look. "How would I know, Mum? It doesn't say stuff like that in the records. It just says like, when she got married and how many kids they had and when she was buried and the like. She had five children in total," he added, "and the second one, a daughter, was our ancestor—and she lived to be eighty-two, which was practically *ancient* then," he said.

"I think she was happy," Sophie said, her voice soft and wistful. "I think she was strong enough to make sure her life was a good one, no matter what happened in it."

Abbie glanced out of the living room window. The edge of the millpond water was just visible from here, shimmering in the watery wintery light.

She smiled. "Me too."

CHAPTER 11
THE RIPPLE EFFECT

"They're here!" John's voice echoed up the stairs excitedly and Abbie practically slammed the lid of her laptop down at once, abandoning their financial records without compunction. Yes, she needed to get the tax forms for the Gobaith Gallery, and *Harpers' Artistic Retreats* finished worryingly soon, but it would always come in second place to a hug from her granddaughter.

She took the stairs far too fast, almost colliding into John in the hallway, and threw open the front door.

"There's my Ellie-Belly!" she beamed, throwing her arms out wide.

Ellie giggled, dashing across the driveway, throwing herself into her Nanna's arms as Abbie swept her up in a tight embrace. The little girl was shooting up like a beansprout, and though she was only five years old, it wouldn't be too long before Abbie couldn't lift her at all.

Sophie rolled her eyes at Dafydd as he negotiated their trunks out of the boot. They were only staying for a week, but it looked like they'd packed for a month.

"You two go and unpack now, and I'll get the kettle on," Abbie said. "You still take it with milk and no sugar, love?"

"Can we have a picnic lunch by the pond, Nanna?" Ellie asked and Abbie laughed, squeezing her granddaughter's hand tightly.

"Of course! You know I can never say no to that."

"You never say no to anything Ellie asks for," Sophie said wryly, lugging their cases up the stairs. "You spoil her far too much."

"If you lived closer, I might spoil her less," Abbie called after her merrily.

It didn't take long for them all to be settled at the edge of the water on an old blanket, happily sharing out a picnic. The lodges and shepherds' huts they'd erected over the mill grounds for the artist retreats they ran were empty this week, and they'd even closed the gallery in honour of the family's arrival, so the whole garden was peaceful and serene. The bright summer sun sparkled off the water's surface merrily, glinting off the two statues that had sat there for nearly fourteen years now. Abbie had ceremoniously erected them on the one-year anniversary of, what they still only ever called, *that night*. The statues still looked just as impressive now as they did when they were first made. In fact, Abbie thought they might be her magnus opus. She doubted she'd ever make something now that could top them. They still drew in crowds for the gallery and the artist retreats they ran here and, though she said it herself, they were becoming something of a local attraction. They sold photograph postcards of them in the heritage centre, even.

She eyed them up with satisfaction. On the edge of the shore was the first of the statues, a black-iron piece she had titled *Community*. There was fear in the tumbling lines of the huddle of amorphous shapes clinging to one another, pulling each other out of the water, and it was a shimmering sharp metal, as dark and deadly as the night itself—but as the strands from each of the strange crunched shapes bound each of them to the other in an unbreakable bond, there was also defiance, hope and justice hidden beneath the surface of that unsettling shape. And there, in the very centre of the lake, made of shards of glittering glass that sparkled like diamonds in the sunny reflection of the water, was its companion piece, *Freedom*. It was tall where first statue was squat, it's shape clear and realistic where the first was impressionistic, its colours as bright and sparkling as the daytime itself, where *Community* seemed to be formed from the very night-time it had been inspired by. *Freedom* was a woman, rising from the waves. Her arms were spread wide, her hair loose and free, a look of peace and triumphant victory beaming from her face as she rose, far above the tumbling mass of huddled figure-like shadows before her. She was victory incarnate.

Abbie liked to think that Catrin would have approved of it. It was a far more fitting tribute than her original frightened shadow sculpture idea would have been.

Beside her, little Ellie, who had already finished off three sandwiches, a cupcake and an orange, was now doodling in a content silence with her colouring pens and an old sketch book of Abbie's.

"She's going to be an artist like Nanna and Grandad," Sophie said, smiling, stroking her daughter's hair softly.

Abbie beamed. Ellie was a good artist already, especially for a five-year-old. Neither Sophie nor Max had shown any interest in arts and crafts at that age, no matter how hard Abbie had tried to encourage them to pursue creative outlets.

"That's wonderful, poppet," she cooed, peeking over Ellie's shoulder. "You can definitely tell it's a man. It looks a bit like a grumpy one though."

"It must be Dafydd then," Sophie smirked, and her husband elbowed her with a grin. "Is it, Ellie? Is it Daddy?"

"Of course not!" Ellie said, very affronted. "Daddy doesn't have hair like that, does he? And he doesn't wear those clothes."

"Oh dear, yes, of course, I can see that now. Sorry," Sophie said hastily with a wink at the others. "Who is it then, Grandad?"

"No, it's the man from the pond," Ellie said stoutly.

The air thickened as silence reigned. Ellie didn't seem to notice the shift in atmosphere, still cheerfully scribbling on the paper before her.

"The woman, you mean?" Sophie said carefully, her voice, perhaps, just a shade higher than it should have been. "The pretty sparkly lady in the middle of the millpond?"

"No, Mummy, the *man*. The one that's stuck there, looking for his niece."

A chill ran over Abbie's skin. She scrabbled to her feet, staring into the waters desperately, but she couldn't see anything. John hurried to stand beside her too, slipping his hand into hers and holding it tightly. It was colder than ice.

The waters were perfectly still. Not a ripple moved them, no strange mists, no disembodied voices. Nothing.

Then the waterwheel creaked.

The End.

ALSO BY CHARLOTTE WEBB

The Haunting of Holly House

The Haunting of Holly House

Meadowbank School for Girls is steeped in history, tradition, and whispers of a dark past.

As the Christmas term draws to a close, excitement buzzes through the boarding house—plays to write, parties to attend, and secrets lurking beneath the surface.

For Lizzy, Rosie, Emma and Dawn the task is simple: choose a prop, create a 20-minute play, and perform it before the school. But when they uncover a dusty Ouija board hidden beneath the stage, their innocent production turns into something far more sinister.

As they dabble with the supernatural, the line between make-believe and reality blurs.

Mysterious messages begin to emerge from the board, eerily connected to Holly House's dark past. Icy chills, unexplainable shadows, and terrifying encounters shake the girls' sense of safety. Strange occurrences aren't just coincidence—something malevolent has awakened.

Flashbacks to 1875 reveal a twisted love affair, a scorned housemistress, and a groundskeeper's dangerous obsession. And as Lizzy unravels the haunting story, she realizes the ghost isn't a stranger at all—it's bound to her by secrets of the past.

In *"The Haunting Of Holly House"* secrets refuse to stay buried, and spirits won't rest until their story is told.

Gripping, atmospheric, and spine-chilling, this supernatural thriller will leave you questioning how far the past can reach into the present—and what happens when it refuses to let go.

Are you ready to discover who—or what—is pushing the glass?

The Lighthouse

The Lighthouse - A Ghost Story

The lighthouse cottage stands on a windswept cliff, surrounded by breathtaking views of sea and sky—a place where time seems to stand still. Its beauty feels almost otherworldly, a tranquil haven far removed from the chaos of modern life. But beneath its serene surface lies something far darker, an unseen force rooted in the cottage's tragic past.

For Emily, the new resident, the ghosts of the past are not just echoes or fleeting memories. They begin as whispers on the wind, cold spots in the cozy cottage, and flickering lights in the dead of night. At first, the disturbances seem harmless, even explainable. But as the weeks pass, they become more invasive, slipping into her dreams and, eventually, her waking life. When the hauntings turn physical, Emily realizes the spirits are not just restless—they're angry.

Sometimes, the ghosts of the past refuse to let go.

ABOUT THE AUTHOR

You are warmly invited to download Charlotte's first, free little book, and to connect with her on Facebook.

Here you can keep up to date with new releases and join in to chat about everything spooky and paranormal.

Ravencross Road (Download for free)

Facebook Page (Please like and follow)

Facebook Group - Charlotte's Haunted House

Charlotte Webb is a gifted author with a passion for all things paranormal. Her love for ghosts and the supernatural led her to run a business in the UK, taking curious thrill-seekers to haunted locations steeped in mystery. With firsthand experiences in some of the country's most eerie sites, Charlotte brings a vivid authenticity to her writing, drawing readers into chilling tales that feel all too real. Her books weave fact and fiction seamlessly, blending her encounters with an imagination that knows no bounds, offering readers a window into the worlds where shadows move, secrets linger, and the past never truly fades away.

Charlotte now resides in an old cottage in a small Northamptonshire village which is steeped in history and holds many ghost stories of its own. She shares her home with her husband, five rescue dogs, four parrots, and a lively flock of chickens and ducks. One of her books is set in this very home, and tells the story of a true ghostly character that has been seen many times in the countryside around her cottage.

Can you tell which is fact or fiction?

Printed in Great Britain
by Amazon